CHAPTER ONE

MAKAYLA TARRANT HAD done some embarrassing things in her twenty-four years on the planet.

Falling off the stage as an awestruck seven-year-old at her first ballet recital? Check.

Flashing a nipple courtesy of a wardrobe malfunction during her stage debut at sixteen? Check.

Stripping in front of sleazy strangers at a dive bar in Kings Cross to ensure her mum had the funeral she deserved? Check.

But nothing came close to the mortification making her muscles spasm as she strutted into the most important audition of her life to date and discovered the casting director was Hudson Watt.

Her best friend growing up.

Her confidant.

Her go-to guy.

The only guy she'd ever really trusted.

Until that night five years ago when he'd seen her naked on stage and her world had imploded.

She hadn't seen him since. Not after the hateful accusations exchanged. He'd misjudged her without giving her a chance to explain. She'd cut him from her life without a second's remorse.

Okay, so that was a lie. At a time when she'd been reeling from her mum's unexpected death, a time when she'd needed her friend the most, a time when she'd done the unthinkable to make sure she could afford a decent funeral, Hudson had morphed into a judgemental monster and she'd lost the best friend she'd ever had.

Back then, she'd pretended she didn't care when in fact she'd grieved for her lost friendship almost as much as for her mum.

'Next,' Hudson said, impatience lacing his tone as he flipped pages on a clipboard.

Makayla didn't move. She couldn't, her feet heavier than her heart as she hovered left stage, wishing she had the guts to turn around and make a run for it before he saw her.

But she needed this job, desperately. Her roommate, Charlotte, was on the verge of leaving and Makayla's pay cheque from working part-time at Le Miel, the hippest patisserie in Sydney, wouldn't cover rent let alone anything else.

She'd auditioned eighteen times for various dance roles over the last few weeks. Nada.

Embue was the coolest nightclub in a city brimming with trendy hotspots and the moment she'd heard they were trialling live shows she'd applied, determined to nail her first dancing role in months. A determination that was rapidly fading when faced with the prospect of dancing for Hudson.

Crap.

What the hell was she going to do?

At that moment, he raised his head and her chance to flee unobserved vanished.

Shock widened his eyes, his lips parting in surprise before compressing into a thin line. A frown slashed his brows. No great surprise he wasn't pleased to see her, considering what she'd called him the last time they'd met.

'Hi, Hudson,' she said, injecting enough fake enthusiasm into her voice to convey nonchalance, but her hand shook as she raised it in a wave. 'Long time no see.'

She inwardly cringed at her blasé, clichéd greeting as she forced her legs to move, heading for centre stage. Where she'd be under the spotlight. Exposed. Vulnerable.

Hell.

After what seemed like an eternity of him pinning her with a laser-like glare, he nodded. 'Mak. So you're auditioning for the lead dancer?'

Mak...only Hudson uttered that one short syllable in a way that touched her deep, like a warm hand strumming her spine in a long languorous caress. His voice seemed lower, huskier, than the last time she'd seen him...when he'd hurled vile assumptions at her and their friendship had crumbled.

'Mak?'

Damn, he'd caught her daydreaming. Now that the option to flee had gone—she wouldn't give him the satisfaction of seeing how rattled she was—she squared her shoulders.

'Yes. I'd love to be lead dancer in Embue's new production. Thanks for the opportunity.'

She didn't give him a chance to respond, shooting the music co-ordinator a quick nod to start her track.

She'd be okay once the song started. The dread making her gut churn would fade. The nerves making her muscles seize would ease. It had to. Because she couldn't fail this audition. Not with so much at stake.

As the first booming bass beat of a Lady Gaga hit blasted from the sound system, an instant wave of calm washed over Makayla.

She could do this.

Music and dance and moving to a rhythm, she understood.

Men who abandoned her when she needed them most, not so much.

As the tempo increased, she began her routine. Steps and twirls and kicks, a high-energy routine designed to dazzle. She let the music take her, her feet pounding to the beat, her arms slicing through the air in perfect synchronisation.

It had always been like this, from the moment she'd seen her mum dance on stage in a nightly Kings Cross revue, a wide-eyed three-year-old mesmerised by the glittery costumes, the make-up and the applause.

She'd adored her mum, had wanted to be exactly like her. Emulating her grace and elegance and vibrancy on stage. But Makayla also wanted more. More kudos. More recognition. More.

Broadway. The pinnacle. Her dream.

But unless she scored a leading role soon, her dream would be in tatters, like her bank account.

The song drew to a close and Makayla threw herself into the finale, a run across the stage complete with high scissor split, before landing nimbly on her feet, arms flung high in victory.

The music cut off, the silence deafening.

At some auditions, she'd seen directors clap for outstanding performances.

Hudson didn't move a muscle.

Swallowing the burgeoning lump in her throat, she stepped to the edge of the stage, out of the spotlight.

He scribbled something down before glancing up at her, his face unreadable.

Her heart sank but she forced a smile. A smile that wavered the longer he stared at her through narrowed eyes.

'We'll be in touch,' he said, and, with a curt nod, dismissed her.

Disappointment made her knees wobble, but she'd be damned if she gave him an insight into her devastation.

Mustering what little courage she had left, she strode offstage.

And flipped him the bird behind the plush gold curtain.

CHAPTER TWO

HUDSON BIT BACK a guffaw.

Mak had flipped him the bird when she thought he couldn't see. But Embue was renowned for its many mirrors and he'd seen her, clear as day, as she'd exited the stage.

Feisty. Bold. Confident. Still the same old Mak. Yet she wasn't the same, not by a long shot.

It had been five years since he'd seen her in that Kings Cross strip club, naked in front of a room of slobbering Neanderthals. Five years since he'd fucked up. Big time.

She'd matured since then, her curves more womanly, her legs a tad longer, her eyes a deeper blue, her hair a rich glorious auburn. She'd always been a stunner growing up but now Mak could knock a guy to his knees and make him grovel to get back up.

When he'd seen her name on the audition sheet, he could've sworn his heart had skipped a beat; she had that kind of impact on him. Always had.

He'd clamped down on his initial reaction to score a line through her name. It wasn't her fault he couldn't erase that night he'd seen her strip and the resultant fallout.

How many times had he picked up the phone afterwards to apologise? To see if she was okay? To talk her out of heading down a nefarious path that he'd seen first-hand resulted in tragedy?

Countless times, when he'd tried to formulate the right words yet had been lacking. He'd wanted to lecture her against the dangers of scoring easy cash via stripping. He'd wanted to warn her of the potential to spiral out of control. He'd wanted to tell her the truth behind his funk in the hope she'd understand why he'd freaked out.

Instead, he'd hung up the phone each and every time, knowing nothing he could say could erase the damage he'd done that night.

He'd said awful things, hateful things, in his shock-induced rage. Sadly, there'd been no coming back from it.

A week later he'd left Kings Cross, moving into a small Manly apartment and into the manager's job at Embue. He'd deliberately avoided going to clubs in the Cross for fear of seeing Mak performing. He couldn't face it, couldn't face seeing her innate innocence tainted in that sleazy world.

Not that he hadn't thought about her over the years. Some women were unforgettable and Mak was one of them.

Seeing her name on his audition sheet had given him a jolt. Could he really face seeing her dance again, when the last time he'd seen her gyrate and shimmy she'd been naked? He feared it would bring back all the old feelings: anger, disgust, with a healthy dose of jealousy. Crazy, out-of-control emotions, when he had no right to feel any of them.

He'd dithered for two days before the agency had called and demanded a list of potential dancers he'd like to trial. Before he could second-guess his decision, he'd added Mak's name to the list.

After seeing what she could do a few minutes ago, he was glad.

Mak could dance. Really dance. Exhibiting the kind of talent that would establish Embue as *the* venue for live shows.

He'd been worried that when she moved on stage, he'd be catapulted back to that horrible night five years earlier and his impartiality as a producer would be shot.

Thankfully, it hadn't happened. He'd been mesmerised by her lithe movement, her ability to command a small space, her stage presence.

Quite simply, as a dancer, Mak was a knockout.

It made him regret all the more that he'd missed out on seeing her come of age the last five years. In a world where he didn't trust easily, Mak had been a good friend. One of the best, next to Tanner.

'Auditions done?' Tanner slumped into the seat next to him and braced his hands behind his head. 'Because Abby is getting angsty with the endless trail of long-legged babes strutting their stuff through here.'

Hudson snorted and placed a thumb in the middle

of Tanner's forehead. 'Your girlfriend is well aware you idolise her and that you're right under this.'

'She's the best.' Tanner swatted away his hand, his friend's goofy grin making Hudson want to puke.

Not that he begrudged his best mate and boss a little happiness. If anyone deserved it, he did, after the shit Tanner had tolerated growing up. But ever since Abby had come on the scene a month ago Tanner had been a shadow of his former self. Staring into space at the oddest of times. Leaving the nightclub early to watch chick-flicks with Abby. Refusing to go out on the town like they used to.

Relationships were for suckers.

Tanner steepled his fingers and rested them in his lap. 'So? Am I wasting my time, giving you a shot at making this live gig fly?'

Hudson sure as hell hoped not. He needed his idea to work. He owed Tanner and he always paid his dues.

'Once I finalise the lead, rehearsals can start.'

Tanner nodded, thoughtful. 'How did Makayla go?'

Hudson startled, immediately followed by a sinking feeling deep in his gut. The kind of feeling that made him want to punch something, preferably Tanner, if he'd slept with Mak.

Women fell at Tanner's feet, always had. Not that Hudson was jealous. He did okay. But the thought of his Mak with anyone…not that she was his. Not any more. Not that she ever had been, really. His outburst that night five years ago had seen to that.

'Mak did well.' Keeping his voice steady with effort, Hudson pretended to study the call-back sheet. 'How do you two know each other?'

Tanner laughed so loud it echoed around the club. 'Man, you should see your face. You look like you've sucked a lemon.'

'Fuck off,' Hudson growled, that urge to thump Tanner growing by the minute.

'I think a more pertinent question is how you know *Mak*?' Tanner's laughter petered to chuckles. 'By your thunderous expression, I'm assuming you know her a hell of a lot better than me.'

'You still haven't answered my question, dickhead.'

Infuriatingly calm and determined to make him sweat, Tanner linked his fingers and stretched forward. 'Makayla works at Le Miel with Abby. So when I filled in there while Remy was in hospital, I got to know her a bit then.'

'Oh.' Hudson deflated in relief, feeling like an idiot for allowing jealousy to cloud his judgement.

He had no right to be jealous of Mak. She could've slept with the entire north shore of Sydney and it still shouldn't bother him. But it did. Deep down in that place where a part of him still missed her dreadfully, he cared. A whole damn lot.

'If you call her Mak, you've known her longer than me?' Tanner's smirk didn't hide his blatant curiosity.

Hudson could lie. But he didn't bullshit Tanner. They'd been through too much together, from the time they were at Kings Cross High, two misfits without mothers, trying to do the best they could with asshole fathers.

'Mak and I go way back,' he said, rubbing the tension cramping his neck muscles. 'When I was working the clubs at the Cross, our paths crossed constantly because her mum danced and waitressed there. We became friends.'

Tanner must've sensed the seriousness behind his declaration, because he stared straight ahead rather than grinning like an idiot. 'How come you never mentioned her back then?'

Because Mak had been all his. The one bright spot in his lousy world. Someone he could confide in, someone who understood the daily battles of growing up in the Cross, because she faced them too.

But he didn't say any of this to Tanner. Instead, Hudson shrugged. 'I didn't want you giving me shit. She's younger than me and I wanted to protect her.'

'A regular Sir Galahad,' Tanner scoffed, the lame-ass grin returning. 'What happened?'

'We had a falling out.' Massive understatement considering the blowout they'd had the night he'd stumbled upon her stripping. 'Haven't seen her in years.'

A speculative gleam made Tanner lean closer. 'So you two haven't...you know?'

'No.'

Not that he hadn't wanted to. But Mak had been off-limits due to her age—and her naivety, if he were completely honest. She'd radiated an innocence that shone bright in an otherwise grimy world. A world of pimps, prostitutes, drugs and strippers. A world he'd worked in out of necessity but had done his damnedest not to let taint him.

It was one of the many reasons he'd flipped out that night he'd seen her gyrating naked on stage.

That, and because of his mum.

'Well, I don't know what's wrong with you, man. Makayla's a bombshell and if I were single I'd take a shot at—'

'Shut the fuck up.'

'Whoa, easy, big fella.' Tanner held up his hands. 'Just giving my opinion. And if you overreact like that to a simple suggestion, I advise you to get laid, pronto.'

Hudson wouldn't give his doofus friend the satisfaction of knowing he wasn't far off the mark. What with getting this show off the ground, he hadn't had time to date lately. In fact, it had to be at least three months since he'd had sex. Maybe that was the reason he'd wanted to bound onto the stage and drag Mak into the nearest dressing room when he'd first seen her up there ten minutes ago?

Yeah, like that was the only reason.

'I need to organise call-backs so if you'll excuse me I've got work to do.' He brandished the clipboard at Tanner, who grinned as if he could see right through his feeble excuse.

'Get laid, buddy. It takes the edge off.' Tanner stood and clapped him on the back. 'According to Abby, Mak hasn't dated anyone in ages, so you two should get *reacquainted*.'

His glare was lost on Tanner as his friend sauntered away, lifting his hand in farewell. Damned if Tanner's advice didn't resonate.

He'd love to put the past behind and move forward

with Mak. But how could he approach her as a friend, when she'd just nailed the lead dancer role in his show?

He might have found his leading lady but once he told her, it ensured they could never be anything but professional.

Mak's talent had floored him. She deserved this role.

So where the hell did that leave him?

CHAPTER THREE

BY THE TIME Makayla made it back to Le Miel to start her shift she'd managed to come up with forty-three different ways she could make Hudson hurt.

Decapitation, evisceration, circumcision…not that she knew if he needed the latter or not, considering they'd never got that far, but she'd be willing to do it without anaesthetic.

His laconic, trite 'we'll be in touch' mocked her, echoing through her head until she'd thumped the steering wheel of her car several times. It hadn't helped. Hopefully, venting to Abby would.

Because if Makayla knew one thing, Hudson wouldn't call her. After the way they'd parted five years earlier, he had no freaking intention of calling her. Ever.

Even if he did, would she accept the job? Could she work with the guy who'd judged her and found her lacking, effectively ending their friendship?

She'd heard the rumours on the entertainment grapevine. That landing the lead gig at Embue could be a good segue into the latest dance extravaganza staging at the Opera House in a few months. And from there...well, dancing at the Sydney icon would look mighty fine on her CV if she ever made it to Broadway.

Broadway...her dream since she'd donned her first tutu and slipped on her first tap shoes.

Growing up, she'd spent countless hours poring over the Internet, watching video clips of shows at the many theatres in midtown Manhattan, wishing she could be a part of it.

Her mum had never scoffed at her dreams. Instead, Julia Tarrant had fostered her love of all things dance, spending every cent she earned on Makayla's dance lessons. It wasn't until her mum had died that Makayla realised the extent of her mum's sacrifice: Julia had no savings, but a detailed record of where her money had gone over the years. A budget that indicated Julia's love for her daughter.

Makayla had adored her mum and discovering she couldn't afford a decent send-off...it had driven her to take drastic action and accept that stripping job for one evening only.

The night Hudson had lost the plot and their friendship had imploded.

'Ugh,' she muttered, knowing she wouldn't be able to stomach her usual *beignet* and cappuccino before she started her shift.

Of all people to audition for, it had to be Hudson.

What the hell was he doing anyway, producing a dance show at Embue? Back then he'd been a gofer for the clubs at the Cross. Doing whatever jobs that came his way. He'd always talked about getting out when he was older, doing something in the club scene, so how did that equate to producing a stage show?

Entering the kitchen, she slammed the back door harder than intended, causing Abby to jump, the pastry brush in her hand clattering to the work bench.

'Sheesh, what's got your knickers in a knot?' Abby waggled a finger. 'Don't you know it takes precision and genius to create the perfect lemon tartlet?'

Makayla rolled her eyes. 'You could make pastries in your sleep and they'd still turn out delish, so quit your moaning.'

'Ouch. Someone's in a mood.' Abby frowned as Makayla slumped onto the nearest stool and scowled. 'Hey, what's wrong?'

'I had an audition this morning. It didn't go well.' Makayla folded her arms, belatedly realising that not even the delicious aromas of cinnamon and sugar wafting from the ovens could lighten her mood today. 'It was a biggie. And I danced my ass off.'

Concern creased Abby's brow. 'And they said no on the spot?'

'Hudson said "we'll be in touch".' She made inverted comma signs with her fingers. 'But I know that's BS.'

'Hudson? I know a guy called—'

'Yeah, he's Tanner's bestie. I didn't know he worked at Embue when I signed up otherwise I wouldn't have auditioned.'

Abby had just answered Makayla's unasked question but she had to be sure. 'You and Tanner didn't have anything to do with me scoring a chance at auditioning for the lead, did you?'

Confused, Abby shook her head. 'I had no idea and I doubt Tanner would, either. He gives his staff free rein while he manages the financial side of things.'

'Thought so.' Makayla slumped further on the stool. She should be happy she'd scored an audition of that calibre on her own. Instead, all she could think about was how she would've landed the role if anyone else had been casting.

'I don't know Hudson well but he seems like a nice guy.'

'He's a prick.'

Not entirely true, and she felt guilty immediately for saying it. Hudson was one of the good guys. At least, he had been until he'd gone berserk, lecturing her and admonishing her when he hadn't had a clue about her motivation for taking off her clothes.

She'd been stunned by the ferocity of his anger. He hadn't given her a chance to explain. He hadn't done much of anything that night he'd watched her strip but lose it backstage, ranting like a madman. She'd been mortified enough at taking off her clothes in front of a roomful of slobbering idiots, but she'd got through it by blocking out the club and everyone in it, and focussing on her mum.

Then Hudson had to dump another shit storm over her at a time she needed his support the most. She'd never forgiven him and had told him so.

Abby wiped her hands and came to sit beside Makayla. 'What happened?'

'Nothing.' She closed her eyes, took a deep breath and opened them. 'Okay, that's not entirely true. Hudson and I were good friends once. Then we weren't any more. And I rocked up today, he was the guy I auditioned for, so it makes sense that's the end of that.'

Abby raised an eyebrow. 'I don't know what happened between you but do you think he's that petty?'

'Who knows?' She snagged her hair and pulled it back into a ponytail. It did little to cool her down. She'd been hot and bothered since she'd strutted out onto that stage at Embue and locked eyes with the devil. 'We didn't exactly part on amicable terms.' She held up her hand. 'And before you ask, shit happens. That's all I'm going to say.'

'Okay.' Abby shot her a sideways glance. 'So what you're saying is you think Hudson won't judge you on your dance ability? That he'll let what happened in your past affect his judgement?' Abby shook her head. 'Doesn't strike me as professional.'

Before Makayla could respond, her cell rang. When she slipped it out of her pocket and glanced at the screen, she didn't know the number.

'I'm waiting on another audition so I need to get this,' she said as Abby nodded, and she hit the answer button. 'Makayla Tarrant speaking.'

'Hey, Mak, it's me.'

Crap. She knew that 'me'.

And he was the last person she'd expected to hear from.

She managed a curt 'hi' before he continued.

'I wanted to let you know that your audition impressed and I'd like you to come in so we can talk.'

She should thank him. Sound enthusiastic. But in that moment, with shock making her gape, all she could think was, I have the opportunity to score a great job working with a not-so-great guy.

'Mak?'

She cleared her throat. 'Sure, I'll come in, thanks. When do you want me?'

Damn, that didn't sound good. But he seemed to think so, as he chuckled. 'Can you meet me back at the Embue studio around seven tonight?'

'Fine,' she said, still surprised by his offer but managing to sound as if she weren't. 'See you then.'

She hit the call end button before he could say anything else to further discombobulate her and stared at the phone as if she couldn't quite believe it.

'Good news?' Abby tapped her on the arm, and Makayla nodded.

'I got a call-back from Hudson.'

'That's great, sweetie.' Abby leaned over and hugged her. 'See? Told you he was a good guy.'

'Yeah…' She sounded less than convinced.

Something in Hudson's tone bugged her. A touch of condescension? Like he was doing her some giant favour. Probably all in her overactive imagination but for a moment she considered calling him back and citing a prior engagement.

Foolishness, considering how badly she needed this job and how it could lead to something much bigger. But she didn't need anyone's pity and she'd be damned if she backed out of this before she'd given it a real shot.

'At the risk of getting my head bitten off, I'm going to offer some advice.' Abby eyeballed her with surprising seriousness. 'Your heart is in dance, not working part-time at a patisserie to pay bills. So whatever happened between you two, forget about it and concentrate on making the most of this opportunity, okay?'

Makayla grunted in acknowledgement. 'Who made you so wise?'

Abby grinned and tapped her temple. 'Considering the mess I made of my own life until recently, guess I learned a thing or two about putting the past behind me.'

'Thanks, Abs.' She leaned over and hugged her friend. 'I've wanted a dance role like this for a long time. So I'll nail this call-back if it kills me.'

The part where she had to meet a guy who'd once been her best friend after hours at a hip club? Not a problem at all.

Not really.

CHAPTER FOUR

HUDSON DIDN'T MAKE it back to the Cross much these days. Not that he shunned his past so much as he'd moved on. But Bluey McNeil had called and when the man who'd given him his first job telephoned, Hudson made an effort.

Bluey hadn't sounded good. In fact, he'd coughed three times during their brief conversation. Hacking coughs that invoked an image of Bluey's packet-a-day habit and how haggard he'd looked the last time Hudson saw him about three months ago.

Foreboding lengthened Hudson's strides as he rounded the iconic El Alamein Fountain, skirted the bar he'd found his father passed out in too many times to count, and into the tiny jazz club aptly named Bluey's after its owner.

While the sun blazed outside, inside the club channelled the darkest midnight, with blackout drapes ensuring the wall sconces glowed and the faux candles created an atmosphere of intimacy. A few patrons dotted tables around the small stage, where a solo saxophonist did his thing. No older than twenty, the kid wasn't bad. And obviously another of Bluey's charity cases, as he'd once been.

'Hey, Squirt, thanks for coming.' A hand clapped him on the back, and Hudson grinned. He'd been a late bloomer, so Bluey had always called him Squirt and the nickname had stuck, even after he shot past six foot at seventeen.

However, when he turned around and caught sight of his friend, Hudson's grin faded. Bluey looked terrible. A walking skeleton. Parchment-thin skin stretched across cheekbones. Furrows bracketing his mouth. And a pallor that indicated just how ill his friend was.

'Any time, you old reprobate.' Hudson enveloped Bluey in a man hug, not surprised that his arms met at the back when they once couldn't. Bluey had lost a shitload of weight and his earlier foreboding blossomed into full-blown panic.

They disengaged, and Bluey gestured at the bar. 'Let's have a seat. What can I get you?'

'The usual,' Hudson said, knowing it got a rise out of his old friend every time.

Bluey's nose wrinkled. 'Orange juice with a spritz of soda is a girl's drink.'

'So you've told me a million times before.' Hudson leaned his forearms on the bar, taking comfort in watching Bluey fill a glass with orange juice and adding a shot of vodka rather than soda, something he'd seen countless times before. 'What's up, old man? Woman troubles?'

Bluey grunted and slid the glass along the bar towards him. 'You've got a big mouth for a whippersnapper. You know my heart belonged to Julia and no woman has come close since.'

'Who's talking about your heart?' Hudson raised his glass in a silent toast, wondering if Mak's mum ever knew about Bluey's crush on her.

This place wasn't just special because of his first boss. Bluey's was the place he'd met Mak, doing homework on a makeshift bench set up in a nook off the main hallway leading to the kitchen, while her mum worked tables. She'd been a beaming fifteen-year-old high on life; he'd been a jaded twenty desperate to get out of the Cross. But there'd been something about her, something refreshing, and once they'd started chatting their friendship had been born.

Back then he'd watched Bluey make puppy dog eyes at Julia, who'd taken it in her stride, as pleasant to Bluey as she'd been to his customers. Everyone had loved Julia and he could've been well on his way to feeling the same for her daughter if he hadn't screwed up so monumentally.

'Listen, Squirt, I've got something to tell you.' Bluey braced himself on the counter behind the bar and Hudson knew the news was bad from the way his eyes darted away. 'I'm heading to the big jazz bar in the sky. Lung cancer. Terminal. Few months left, tops.'

Hudson's stomach fell away, and he downed the orange and vodka in two gulps as Bluey continued. 'I wanted you to hear it from me, not by a second-hand phone call after one of the geezers here rang to invite you to my funeral.'

Hudson wanted to say something, anything, to

make this better. He remained silent, anger and regret roiling in his gut alongside the vodka.

'And before you go getting all sentimental on me, stop.' Bluey thumped his fist against the bar. 'I've been around for sixty-one years and been lucky enough to run this place for most of it. So don't feel sorry for me. I've had a good inning. And enjoyed sucking back on each and every one of those bloody cancer sticks that gave me this bugger of an illness.' He thumped his chest. 'So now you know. What's happening with you?'

The ache of impending loss blossomed in Hudson's chest. He'd experienced the same feeling before, the night he'd strode into Le Chat and seen Mak stripping on stage. In that moment he'd laid eyes on her, wearing a thong and little else, he'd known they were over.

And when she'd removed that thong…there'd been no coming back from that, and he grieved the loss of their friendship almost as much as he'd grieved the mother he'd never known.

This time he waited until the ache eased. Took his time formulating a response. If he'd done the same thing with Mak back then, maybe they would've had a chance.

When the lump in his throat finally subsided, Hudson said, 'Thanks for telling me but damn, it's fucked up.'

'Yeah, Squirt, it is, but what's a man to do?' Bluey shrugged and blinked rapidly. 'Tell me something to take my mind off it.'

'Mak auditioned for me today.' The words tripped out in haste and he instantly regretted them because if he'd cottoned on to Bluey's crush on Julia the old guy definitely noticed his on Mak and had teased him endlessly about it.

'How's she doing?'

'Good.' Hudson ignored the knowing glint in Bluey's astute gaze. 'She's got talent. I'm casting her as the lead dancer in the revue I'm producing at Embue.'

'Well, well, well.' Bluey folded his arms, his grin smug. 'This should be interesting.'

'We'll be working together in a professional capacity,' he said, sounding like a pompous ass and hoping he could keep it that way.

He needed to delineate clear boundaries from the start: he would be Mak's boss, she'd need to follow his orders. He couldn't afford to blur lines. Not when he had no frigging idea how he'd go seeing her dance for him every single day. Just because he'd coped at her audition didn't mean he had a grip on his memories.

Seeing her dance for those few minutes already had him thinking about her way too much and imagining how their future interactions would go, professional or otherwise.

Bluey sniggered. 'I have no idea why you two fell out and I haven't seen that darling girl in years but you tell her I said hi. And if you've got half a brain in that big head of yours, you'll treat her right this time.'

'What do you mean, this time?'

Bluey rolled his eyes. 'Because, numbskull, it's always the man's fault, and if you haven't figured that out by now, you're thicker than I thought.'

Hudson managed a wry grin. 'I'm going to miss you.'

'Right back at you, kid.' Bluey's eyes glistened before he turned away to cough, the harsh sound raising the hairs on the back of Hudson's neck.

Life wasn't fair. He'd figured that out pretty damn early when his mum did a runner and he was left in the custody of a mean drunk. But losing Bluey would hit hard and he knew it.

When Bluey's cough petered out, he turned back around. 'Now get the hell out so I can do some work.'

'Propping up the bar, you mean?' Hudson stood, moved around the bar, and enveloped him in another hug. 'You call me, okay? Any time, day or night, if you need anything.'

'Thanks, kid.' Bluey shoved him away with half-hearted force. 'You always were a soft touch.'

Not always. Hudson had taken a hard stand with Mak and look how that had turned out.

'I'll pop in next week,' he said, and Bluey saluted in response, his mouth downturned and worry clouding his eyes.

Bluey had said he had months to live but with a death sentence hanging over him, Hudson understood the old guy would be living each day as his last.

The injustice of it all swamped him anew and he headed for the door, desperate for air before he bawled. He stumbled outside, and it took a while until his eyes adjusted to the sudden glare and he made for the nearby fountain, slumping onto a bench next to it.

Tourists streamed by, snapping pics with their phones or giggling excitedly about being in Australia's most notorious suburb.

To him, Kings Cross would always be home in a way no one could understand unless they'd lived here. Unless they'd braved the back streets. Unless they'd used every ounce of savviness to survive.

Mak understood. And catching up with Bluey had clarified his situation with her in a way he could never have anticipated.

Life was too short to hold on to the past. Ironic, he'd strived so hard to become successful and put the past behind him yet here he was, back where it all started, feeling as lost and lonely as he had back then.

He'd come a long way. Mak probably had, too. He had no right to judge her. Not any more.

When she came in tonight, he'd keep an open mind. Be friendly. Try to forget the past and focus on the future.

They both deserved that.

CHAPTER FIVE

MAK STRODE INTO Embue as if she owned the place, confident that she'd achieved the impression she'd aimed for and then some.

Smoky eyes. Siren-red lips. Sleek blow-dried hair. Killer heels. And a strapless, knee-length, figure-hugging emerald sheath that had got her more second dates than she could count.

Earlier today, auditioning for Hudson had rattled her. Tonight, she wanted to assert her dominance and show him who was boss.

A tad overdramatic, maybe, and in reality she'd have to be deferential and respectful because she really needed this job. But dressing like this ensured she felt good and the way her insides quivered with nerves she needed all the help she could get.

Her mum had taught her many life lessons, and dress to impress had been one of them. It didn't matter whether she was doing a yoga class early on a Saturday morning or picking up groceries on her way home, she always wore lipstick and mascara. She felt naked without them. And while her budget might be verging on dire, she managed to find outfits at second-hand shops that garnered compliments.

As she caught sight of herself in one of the many mirrors lining the club, she squared her shoulders and stood tall. She could do this. Meet with Hudson. Convince him to hire her. Dance her ass off for however long this show ran. Definitely doable.

Until she caught sight of him striding towards her, and her tummy went into free fall, her confidence following suit.

This was Hudson.

The guy she'd secretly crushed on for years.

The guy she'd idolised.

The guy who'd been the best friend a girl could wish for.

The guy who'd seen her stark naked, at her most vulnerable, and turned his back on her.

Crap.

'Hey, Mak, glad you could make it.' He held out his hand, like it was the most natural thing in the world they shake in greeting, when it had once been customary for them to exchange a kiss on the cheek. 'Let's head into the studio to talk.'

Mak managed a mute nod, surreptitiously swiping her palm against the side of her dress when he released it. Yeah, like that would stop the tingles creeping up her arm.

It had been years since she'd seen him, so why the same irrational reaction, as if her body recognised on some visceral level what her brain refused to acknowledge?

She should hate him for how he'd treated her, how he'd dismissed their friendship without a second thought. But she couldn't afford to let her residual bitterness towards him flare now. This job had to come first.

'How was your day?' He cast her a sidelong glance, as if he couldn't gauge her mood. Join the club. She didn't have a clue how to act around him now that her faux confidence had dwindled on sight.

'Same old,' she said with a shrug. 'I work part-time at a patisserie. Le Miel. You may have heard of it?'

Of course he had, considering his boss Tanner had worked there temporarily while his brother Remy had been laid up in hospital following a fall. And Abby knew him, which meant he'd know she worked there, too. But she wanted to see how honest he'd be, how their new working relationship would pan out from the start.

He was staring at her as if he knew she'd been trying to trip him up somehow. 'Tanner's my best bud, so yeah, I know it. And I've met Abby, she's lovely.'

Relieved he'd been honest, she nodded. 'They're both good people.'

He cast her a quizzical look. 'Are you okay?'

No, she wasn't. She couldn't do this. Couldn't pretend they didn't have a past. Like the argument that had ruined their friendship never happened. Like she wasn't still hurting that he'd thought so little of her; that he hadn't known her as well as she'd thought he did.

'Honestly? I'm having a hard time accepting you as my potential boss considering we share a past.'

He didn't react. In fact, she couldn't see a flicker of acknowledgement on his stoic face bar a slight clenching of his jaw. How did he do that? Hold his emotions so closely in check when she was having a hard time not blurting every single thing she wanted to say to him?

'Let's talk in here.' He pushed the double doors to the studio open and waited until she'd passed through before closing them.

Makayla should've relaxed stepping into the studio with its familiar set-up of stage, mirrors, steel rails lining the walls and spotlights. The space was new, or rarely used, because it didn't have the familiar smell of stale sweat and greasepaint. Maybe that explained her nerves.

A crock and she knew it. Her nerves had everything to do with the man staring at her with trepidation, as if he knew she was about to unleash years' worth of home truths.

Before she could speak, he held up his hand, annoyingly imperious. 'I know we need to talk about what happened back then. But before we do, I want you to know you've got the job of lead dancer. Your audition blew me away and I'm not saying that out of some warped case of guilt because of how things ended between us, I'm saying it because you're incredibly talented and I need this show to succeed, so I want you in it.'

He blew out a long breath after his ramble and in that moment she realised he was nervous, too. Hudson didn't do long-winded speeches. Less was more for him when it came to words. So the fact he'd blurted all that indicated he was just as nervous as she was.

'Thanks, I'm thrilled to get the job.' She sounded formal, stilted, and cleared her throat, wondering how long she'd have the job for once she said what needed to be said. 'But the last time we saw each other you basically called me a whore and it's difficult getting past that.'

He flinched as if she'd struck him. 'I didn't—'

'You didn't use the word but it was pretty damn clear from everything else you said what you thought of me.'

That night was imprinted on her brain. The night she'd been so desperate to give her mum the funeral she deserved that she'd shelved her principles and done whatever it took to get the money she needed.

Hudson hadn't given her a chance to explain. He'd taken one look at her stripping on stage and flipped out. She'd expected better from her best friend. She'd expected so much more than what she'd got.

While time should've eased her resentment it hadn't, and seeing him again seemed to bring it all back in a mortifying rush.

She remembered every single moment of that humiliating night in excruciating detail. Pretending not to care when the club owner leered at her, demanding she strip down to bra and panties so he could see the goods before he gave her the gig. Throwing up before she went on stage. The stench of cheap aftershave and beer when she'd been taking her clothes off.

And in the midst of her degradation, she'd spotted Hudson, staring at her as if she were the worst person in the world.

His opinion mattered to her. *He* mattered to her and having him witness her shameful, demeaning show had crushed her. She'd been desperate to explain. He hadn't let her. His appalling lecture had rung in her ears long after he'd stormed out.

Now she had to dredge all that up so they could move forward as professionals. Ugh.

'I'm sorry.' He leaned against the nearest wall, looking like a cool, impervious model, not a guy hell-bent on repentance. 'That was the night I landed the job at Embue and I came looking for you to share my good news. Bluey told me he'd seen you entering Le Chat so I headed there.' He shook his head, remorse twisting his mouth. It was an improvement on the loathing she'd seen all those years ago. 'I freaked out. Said some things I shouldn't have—'

'You were my best friend! You should've trusted me.' She swallowed down the lump of emotion lodged in her throat, making her voice embarrassingly squeaky. 'I didn't owe you any explanations then and I sure as hell don't owe you any now, but that was the worst night of my life and having you witness my mortification, then berate me for it, sucked big time. Then you turned your back on me...'

Damn, if she didn't wind this up soon she'd end up crying and that wasn't the professional impression she wanted to present.

'Maybe it was for the best, us moving on with our lives separately, leaving the Cross behind, but there isn't a day that goes by that I don't miss the friendship we once had.' There, she'd said it, though she ended on an embarrassing half hiccup that had her wishing the ground would open up.

Hudson didn't say a word. He just stared at her, sadness down-turning his mouth, before he crossed the short space between them and enveloped her in a hug that squeezed the air from her lungs.

She resisted for a moment, not wanting the physical contact, not wanting anything from him bar this job. But this was Hudson, the guy she'd depended on almost as much as her mum, and if her brain resisted her body had other ideas. His arms were strong around her, crushing her like a steel band, his warmth staving off the chill that had invaded her bones around the time they'd started this conversation.

Breathless, she finally relaxed into him, and as if sensing her capitulation, he hugged her tighter if that were possible. It should've ended there. An apologetic embrace between two old friends who'd been torn apart in the past but now had to work together.

Instead, she felt the shift between them, the exact moment the hug became something else. His woodsy aftershave, something expensive, probably designer, made her nose tingle. His warmth turned to heat where it pressed against her. His hand splayed in her lower back, grazed the top of her ass. Something semi-hard nudged her hip.

He pulled away but didn't release her, as she tilted her head up. 'I'm not proud of the way I treated you that night and I've regretted losing our friendship over it. But I care about you, Mak, I always have, so if you'd let me I'd like to be friends again.'

He sounded sincere and his eyes blazed with untold emotion, but she couldn't forget how badly he'd once hurt her. If young Hudson had had the power to do that, the older, sexier version would be a lot more dangerous if she let him get close again.

'We can try,' she said, sounding flippant, but still caught up in the weird unspoken tension shimmering between them. 'I'm a professional and I intend on making the most of the opportunity you've given me.'

'I wasn't talking about work and you know it,' he said, his low voice rippling over her like a caress, making her all too aware she hadn't pulled out of his arms yet.

She should. She should establish a clear boundary between them from the outset, but when his burning gaze dropped to her mouth and her nipples hardened in response she knew it would take more than putting space between them to reinforce all they shared was a working relationship.

She'd always been like this around him, hyper-aware, like her body was somehow invisibly, intrinsically attuned to his. He hadn't known back then; she'd been too good at hiding it. It should've dissipated over the years, disappeared completely, but the longer he stared at her with blatant hunger, the harder she found it to remember why she had to maintain distance from him.

'We can try the friendship thing,' she said, finally willing her legs to move and breaking free of his embrace by backing away a few steps. 'But I'll give you a heads-up. I'm not the same naive girl I once was.'

'And I'm not the same narrow-minded jerk I once

was.' His lopsided grin catapulted her back in time to the many times that same smile had made her young, impressionable heart beat faster. 'Now we've established we've both grown up, shall we talk business?'

'Absolutely.' Her emphatic nod sent her hair tumbling over her shoulders and she pushed it back, a simple, innocuous action with complicated results when Hudson's gaze locked on her hair as if he wanted to bury his face in it.

Hell. She could do friendship in a pinch but anything more between them would be disastrous. He might not know it but he'd given her a big break professionally in hiring her for this lead dancer role. She couldn't screw it up. She wouldn't. No matter how much intrigue spurred her on to see exactly how hot Hudson was beneath that cool facade.

'Tell me about the show,' she said, sounding fake and upbeat and perky, while she couldn't ignore the way heat flared inside at the way he stared at her like he'd been given the keys to his favourite ice-cream store.

He eyeballed her and in that moment she saw he faced the same inner battle she did. Lust versus logic. Curiosity warring with common sense. Desire battling deprivation.

Crap. She might have just landed a dream job but she had a feeling she'd landed neck-deep in a load of trouble, too.

'Tell me about you first.' He gestured at a bar stool, indicating she sit. She didn't want to. She wanted to stand so she could make a run for it if she needed to.

Because being in Hudson's arms had resurrected a whole host of feelings she'd long suppressed. She should hate him for how he'd treated her and their friendship. Instead, she'd accepted his apology, even though he hadn't explained why he'd behaved so appallingly towards her, and agreed to try the friendship thing now.

Was she insane?

'Not much to tell.' She perched on the edge of the stool, ready to flee at the slightest sign of awkwardness. 'I attended uni for a while, doing a bachelor of applied dance in the hope I could teach as well as perform. But I hated the rigidity of classes so lasted less than six months.'

His eyebrows rose, as if he couldn't believe she'd even consider a career in teaching. 'I can't imagine you being an instructor.'

She instantly bristled. 'Why not?'

'Because you've always had talent and haven't you heard the old cliché, those who can do, those who can't teach?'

Assuaged by his compliment, she continued. 'Guess I'm a cliché then, because once I focussed on dancing, I never looked back.'

'The agency sent across the CVs of all applicants auditioning.' He hesitated. 'You've had tons of experience but no starring roles?'

Damn him for homing in on her weakness.

'What's with the twenty questions?' She sounded snappish and didn't care.

He was her boss, she was his employee, that was

where it ended. She didn't need him treating her like a friend catching up for old times' sake. It blurred lines and she preferred perfectly delineated boundaries. She couldn't deal with anything else, not now, when seeing him again had resurrected so many feelings, many of them bad.

'Because I want to know what makes you tick these days.' He reached out and touched her above her heart. 'In here.'

It had been nothing more than a fleeting brush of his fingertips against her skin; a barely there touch that shouldn't have mattered. But it did, because heat flooded her body, most of it ending up in her cheeks.

'I said I'd try the friendship thing. Don't push it,' she said, easing him away with her index finger.

He laughed, the same rich, deep sound she remembered and damned if she didn't prickle with awareness. Everywhere.

'Friends ask about each other's interests. They chat. They tease—'

'No teasing.'

It was one of the things she'd loved most about him back then, his ability to make her laugh.

'You used to love it when I taunted you.' He leaned forward as if to prove it, invading her personal space, his mouth mere inches from her ear. 'Just because we haven't seen each other in years doesn't mean I've forgotten anything.'

Damn.

Did he know how she'd felt back then? Was that why he was torturing her now?

Though it was more than two friends getting reacquainted and she knew it. There was a sexual tension between them, simmering beneath the surface, deliberately ignored but there all the same.

Not good.

'Then you'll remember how much I hated you bugging me when I was doing homework and not much has changed.' She elbowed him away, and he clutched at his side in mock outrage. 'I'm your employee. I need to focus, not be distracted by…by…you,' she finished lamely, not wanting to articulate exactly how badly the ever-present attraction between them was making her lose focus and her cool.

'You find me distracting?' His low voice made it sound like she'd found him naked.

'I find you painful.'

Her dry response made him laugh again. 'Tell me you don't feel more comfortable now than when you first came in?'

So that was what he'd been doing. Trying to put her at ease. She should've been relieved. Instead, a familiar mortification in his presence swamped her; had she imagined the attraction between them?

His boner during their hug could've meant nothing, a simple physiological reaction guys got when in close proximity with a woman. And his banter could've been exactly as he'd said, a way to put her at ease.

To her chagrin, he squeezed her hand, like a friend would do.

'Look, Mak, we have to work together. I think it's great we've confronted the past and reached a point where we can talk like this. It'll make the next few weeks a hell of a lot easier.'

He was right, of course. While they couldn't resume their old friendship, they had to be civil.

But he hadn't released her hand, and as she stared at it, his strong tanned fingers wrapped around hers, she couldn't help but think that for a guy who professed friendship, he'd been teetering on the brink of overstepping the mark.

As if to reinforce it, his thumb brushed across the back of her hand in a slow, languorous sweep that made her tingle and bite back a moan.

Hell.

She could do friendship with Hudson.

Anything else could only end in disaster.

CHAPTER SIX

HUDSON COULDN'T HAVE been more relieved to see the entire dance cast troop into the studio five minutes later, after he'd given Mak a brief rundown of her duties in the show.

The longest frigging five minutes of his life.

He'd always been attracted to her but now…fuck, he got hard again just thinking about that moment when she'd been in his arms, her lithe body pressed against him, her familiar exotic fragrance befuddling his senses.

She'd worn that perfume for as long as he could remember. One of the dancers in the club her mum had worked at had brought it back from Hong Kong for her and damned if he wanted to know how she still managed to get her hands on more.

Had she travelled? Worked overseas? Had a boyfriend obtained more from there? So many questions he had no answers to and it irked that he knew so little about her when he'd once known everything.

Or so he'd thought.

He was glad they'd cleared the air. As much as

could be expected, that was. He hadn't told her why he'd freaked out that night he'd caught her stripping and she hadn't told him why it had been the most mortifying night of her life.

He'd wanted to ask. Hell, he wanted to know what drove her to it when she'd been ingenuous and sheltered despite growing up in the sin capital of Australia.

But prying wouldn't have served any good, not when they had to work together. He'd tried to put her at ease, to ask innocuous questions, but she'd been defensive and wary. He didn't blame her, considering how their friendship had ended. But he wanted some semblance of their old camaraderie now so they could at least work together and not have to deal with old wounds.

He'd invited her over earlier than the other cast members to smooth things over between them. He'd succeeded to a point but having Mak look at him with anything other than loathing only served to remind him how much he wanted her and, unfortunately, his dick had no problem keeping up with the programme.

He'd touched her, several times. More to prove to himself that his reaction to having her in his arms had been an aberration, his body's way of telling him to get laid sooner rather than later.

It hadn't been, because even with a simple handhold, he'd felt *it*, that insistent tug of attraction that grabbed him by the balls and wouldn't let go.

A major problem, considering Mak was his lead dancer and he was her boss, not to mention they both carried enough baggage to fill an airport carousel.

'See you at rehearsals Monday, boss.' The lead male, a short guy named Shane, clapped him on the back with an overfamiliarity that set his teeth on edge.

But Hudson forced a smile and nodded. 'Have a good weekend.'

The rest of the eight-person crew filtered out. Everyone except Mak, who had vanished. Surely she wouldn't have snuck out without saying goodbye?

The thought saddened him and just as he'd poured his first bourbon from the makeshift bar in the corner, she slipped back into the room, her eyes widening in surprise as she noted it had emptied.

'Where is everyone?'

'Gone home to start their weekends early.'

She glanced at her watch. 'It's eight-thirty.'

'Early by clubbing standards.'

'I know that.' She rolled her eyes as she padded towards him, having discarded her stilettos ages ago. 'I'll have you know I'm the dance queen of Sydney.'

He liked her haughty playfulness, remembered her often throwing out challenges to best him. 'There's a difference between dancing for a living and burning up the floor for fun.'

'I'm the best at both.' Her chin tilted as she stared him down. 'Single in Sydney means let the good times roll.'

Grinning, he said, 'We're still talking about dancing, yeah?'

She snickered, a cute sound that catapulted him back in time. 'You're such a guy.'

'Glad you noticed.' He flexed his biceps, garnering a dry chuckle. 'Because I'm single in Sydney and

I can guarantee that whenever I get anywhere near a dance floor my right foot morphs into my left, so I have two of them.'

She muttered something that sounded like 'bullshit' under her breath, before flashing him a teasing smile he hadn't seen in forever. 'As I recall, whenever you were working the Kings Cross clubs you'd manage to squeeze in a boogie and trust me, your moves were far from a guy with two left feet.'

'You kept an eye on me? I'm touched.' He clutched his chest, thrilled that they'd reverted to swapping banter as they used to. It was what he'd been aiming for earlier but she hadn't responded, too guarded as she'd tried to get a read on him.

Now that she'd loosened up, he hoped they could continue in the same vein. It had been so natural back then, teasing each other like this, sharing laughs. He'd missed this light-hearted fun the most.

'You know all the girls had a crush on you back then.'

'Even you?' He leaned on the bar, trying to appear casual when he wanted her answer to be affirmative too much.

'I had more sense,' she said with a nonchalant shrug, but not before he glimpsed the cheeky spark in her eyes.

Yeah, the old Mak was back and he couldn't be happier. 'Would you like a drink?'

She hesitated, her gaze drifting to the door a second before she surprised him and nodded. 'Vodka and lemon, please.'

'Coming right up.' He didn't need to measure out the quantities. He'd helped out behind bars since he could practically walk and he found the familiar action soothing. Or maybe that had more to do with Mak watching his every move.

He should've found her scrutiny off-putting. He didn't. Instead, her presence had a calming effect, the way it always had.

Back then she'd steadied him in a topsy-turvy world he'd rallied against with every fibre of his being. He'd done whatever it took to survive, saving every cent he'd earned from odd jobs to formulate a plan to escape the life that had threatened to drag him down.

These days, he spent way too much money on caring for the man who'd done his best to make his life hell, but the way he saw it, paying for his father's care facility kept the old bastard away from him. When he saw him, it was on his terms. Just the way he liked it.

'What's wrong?' She perched on a bar stool and rested her chin in her hands, studying him. 'You look sad. Are my lame jokes at your expense that bad?'

He shook his head, impressed she could still read him so well. 'Just thinking about Dad.'

Wariness clouded her eyes. Like most people who lived at the Cross back then, she'd known Wiley Watt was a deadhead drunk and a mean prick. 'How is he?'

'Dementia claimed him a few years ago. Drifts in and out. He's in a private facility.'

Before she could say anything else he changed the subject, not wanting to taint their reawakening friendship by discussing the one subject he'd rather avoid at all costs. 'I saw Bluey today.'

Her eyes lit up and for a ridiculous second jealousy stabbed him as he wished she'd look at him like that. 'Haven't seen him in years. How is he?'

Damn, when he'd wanted to change the subject, he'd grabbed at the first thought that popped into his head. Not the smartest move, considering that brightness in her eyes would fade the moment he divulged the truth.

'He has lung cancer. Terminal. Few months tops.' He slid her drink towards her, and when she slumped he felt like he'd revealed there was no Santa. 'But he's happy. Brash as ever. Wanted me to hear it from him and not get a call for his funeral.'

'That's Bluey,' she said, blinking rapidly, as he quelled his first instinct to bundle her in his arms. 'He was so cute, the way he mooned over Mum.'

'Did she know?'

'Of course.' A soft smile of remembrance played about her mouth. 'But Mum was too smart to mix business with pleasure.'

She eyeballed him as she said it, a clear warning he should heed. But damned if keeping his hands off her wouldn't be the hardest thing he'd done in a long time.

'Smart woman, your mum,' he said, taking a slug of his bourbon. 'You must miss her.'

'Every single day.' She downed two thirds of her vodka in one gulp. 'That's what I hated most after you weren't around any more because I'd just lost Mum. And not having my best friend there to bounce ideas and feelings off, the kind of friend who moved in the same circles, the friend who knew me almost better than I knew myself…'

She trailed off and for a horrifying moment he thought she might burst into tears.

Before he could say anything remotely comforting, she tossed back another gulp of vodka. 'Don't mind me. It's the alcohol loosening my tongue and making me maudlin.'

'I missed us too,' he blurted, wishing he hadn't said anything when she stared at him in hope as she used to.

Back then he'd known he couldn't be Mak's hero, no matter how much he wanted to. He wasn't built that way. He'd learned from a young age to take care of number one and that was him.

He hadn't fostered anything beyond friendship between them because of it, even after Mak had turned eighteen. It would've been so easy to slip into a relationship with her, especially considering how much he'd wanted her.

But he'd known he wasn't the kind of guy Mak deserved, not the kind of guy she wanted. Not really. Mak craved stability and he could never give that to her. Not after what he'd been through. Pushing her away that night he'd seen her strip had almost been a relief in some ways.

Now she was back. Tugging at his heartstrings all over again. Making him want to slay a goddamn arena full of dragons in order to protect her from bad stuff.

Not good.

He was a different man now. He'd moved on from that guy who'd felt unworthy. But he still couldn't be her guy. He had too many demons, most of them linked to that night he'd seen her strip, a night he might never get past no matter how close they became.

'Here's to us,' she said, raising her almost empty glass. 'To friendship.'

Friendship he could do. Contemplating anything else would be beyond madness.

'To friendship.' He clinked his glass against hers but when he took a slug of bourbon it burned all the way down his throat, testament to the lie he'd just uttered.

He didn't just want friendship with Mak. He wanted *her*. He always had.

In his arms. In his bed. Wrapped around him.

It was going to be one hell of a tough time ahead.

CHAPTER SEVEN

MAKAYLA DIDN'T BELIEVE in magic. Not since she'd watched a show backstage as a ten-year-old and discovered the magician was merely good at fooling people into believing what they wanted to believe.

But someone had sure sprinkled a handful of fairy dust over her today because she'd never danced so well. Rehearsal had started at five p.m. Monday and she'd been at it for two hours. Feet flying, legs kicking, arms spinning. Nailing every single move. The dancers around her were good—it looked as if Hudson only hired the best—but today, she was better.

She didn't get it. Usually when she landed a new role it took her a day or two to pick up the rhythms, to trial the steps, until it clicked. Today, from the moment she'd stepped onto the studio stage at Embue and the choreographer had outlined the major moves, she'd been on fire.

Now, with sweat pouring off her and her damp leotard clinging to her skin, she slumped onto the nearest bench and reached for her drink bottle. Maybe it was something in the water. Or maybe it was dancing for the man heading towards her, admiration making his eyes glow indigo.

'Wow, that was impressive.' Hudson sat beside her, his thigh almost brushing hers, and she forced herself to relax. 'You're good.'

'Tell me something I don't know,' she said, raising her water bottle to him in a mock toast before downing half of it.

He chuckled. 'What do you think of the show?'

She was paid to dance, not give an opinion, but she liked the fact he'd asked. 'It's great. High energy, good tempos, catchy songs.'

'I've been working part-time in local theatre, behind the scenes mostly, for a while. It's something of a hobby.' Concern pinched his mouth, at odds with his usual confidence. Even as a guy in his early twenties doing whatever it took to survive he'd had a cockiness about him, a self-assurance that she'd wished she could emulate. 'Tanner's never done anything like this at Embue before. He took a chance on my idea. I need it to rock.'

'It will,' she said, instinctively patting his thigh in reassurance before belatedly realising she'd made a dumb move.

Being attracted to her boss was one thing. Touching him entered a whole other stratosphere of stupidity.

His muscle flexed beneath her palm and she snatched it away before insanity prevailed and she slid her hand higher.

'With your talent, why haven't you had any long-term roles?'

She appreciated his switch back to business-like. That impulsive gaff with her hand had been beyond embarrassing. 'Not for lack of trying.'

She picked up a towel, draped it across the back of her neck and dabbed at her face with it. 'I bust my butt attending auditions. I get countless call-backs. But the big roles seem to elude me.'

'But you're phenomenal.' He sounded a tad awe-struck, confusion creasing his brow, and she smiled.

'Thanks.' She bumped him with her shoulder, wishing she could hug him for his rousing endorsement. 'I'm hoping being the primary dancer in this show will lead to bigger things.'

'Like?'

She hadn't articulated her dream out loud to many people for fear of being laughed at. But Hudson had connections. She'd done some online research after she'd landed the lead dancer role and discovered he did a lot of theatre stuff in addition to his management job here at the club that ensured he'd meet a lot of influential people. If he had contacts in the industry, he might be able to help.

But before she could say anything, he snapped his fingers. 'How could I forget? You always wanted to be on Broadway. Is that still your goal?'

Heat flushed her cheeks that he'd remembered something so trivial and she nodded. 'Sounds far-fetched, huh? But it's been my end goal since I started dancing as a kid. I want the bright lights. The big stage. In the most happening city in the world…'

She trailed off, lost in her musings as she usually

was whenever she thought of New York City and how utterly fabulous it would be to visit, let alone live and perform there.

'From what I've seen today, you're good enough to get there and then some,' he said, staring at her in frank admiration. 'You've got the moves, kid, the kind that could take you all the way.'

She resisted the urge to preen under his praise; that and fling herself at him in gratitude. Usually, she didn't need other people inflating her ego; she was a realist and knew she had talent that could flourish given time, effort and the right environment. She'd been lucky enough to have two of the best dance teachers in the biz growing up and they'd never minced words. Giving praise when it was due. Kicking her in the butt when she needed it.

But having Hudson praise her meant something and she knew why. She'd always valued his opinion. Had sought it out, from his views on her latest lip-gloss colour to upcoming pop bands. Despite their five-year age difference, he'd never made her feel stupid or inept. He'd listened to her; truly listened, then offered sage advice. Yet another thing she'd missed when their friendship ended, not having a sounding board she trusted.

'Hey, did I say something wrong?' He touched her arm, a brief impersonal touch that sent a jolt all the way down to her toes.

'No, just thinking how much I appreciate having your input again.' She grabbed the end of her towel and swatted him with it. 'But careful, I might get a big head with all that flattery.'

'You're too grounded for that, always have been,' he said, batting away the towel. 'I think that's one of the things that drew me to you back then. Low tolerance for BS, you saw the world how it was yet it didn't get you down.' Something akin to darkness, a fleeting shadow, clouded his eyes. 'Growing up in the Cross was tough but you took it in your stride and didn't let it taint you.'

'Yeah, I did,' she said, remembering the one night when she'd succumbed to the seedier side of Kings Cross and why.

She could've let the memory of that degrading night drag her down but she hadn't. She'd taken the money and walked away without looking back.

She could've taken the easy option and done more strip shows. That one night, she'd earned more than dancing two months' worth of gigs. The owner had offered her a sizeable pay, enough to set her up. But she'd knocked it back for the reason Hudson had articulated: she hadn't wanted to be tainted by the kind of life she didn't want.

She'd never regretted it but she couldn't help but wonder at times how much easier her life could've been if she'd had that kind of money as a nineteen-year-old.

Hudson stared at her, a host of unasked questions hovering between them, before he blinked and glanced away. 'I don't do anyone favours unless they deserve them but if what I saw today is any indication of what you can do on stage, I'll keep my ear to the ground. Let you know if I hear of any big opportunities here in Sydney, maybe even overseas, okay?'

'Thanks, that would be great.' This time, she didn't hesitate in wrapping her arms around him in a grateful hug. It felt right, comfortable, and nothing like the tension-fraught comforting hug last week. 'Anyone ever tell you you're the best boss ever?'

'Only every single day,' he said, his smile bashful when she released him. 'Speaking of work, I better get back out there otherwise Tanner will fire my ass for slacking off on my management duties.'

'And I've got an appointment for a one-off show.' She glanced at her watch and leapt to her feet. 'Crap. I didn't know rehearsal ran overtime. I'm going to be late.'

She glanced at her drenched workout gear and grimaced. 'No time to head home for a shower. You don't have one around here that staff can use, by any chance?'

Hudson hesitated, a flash of something indefinable in his stare, before he huffed out a breath, as if he'd come to some momentous decision. 'I live in the apartment over the club. You're welcome to shower there if it makes things easier for you.'

A ripple of awareness made her skin prickle. She couldn't turn up for a dress fitting for another show sweaty and flustered; or worse, late. But taking advantage of Hudson's generous offer meant getting flustered in another way entirely.

Standing in his shower stall, imagining him in there, soapy and slick and naked…

'Uh, thanks, that would make life easier,' she said, clearing her throat when her voice sounded a tad high. 'I appreciate the offer.'

'No worries,' he said, waiting until she gathered her stuff before heading for the door.

Easy for him to say, she thought as she followed him. Because getting a glimpse into Hudson's home life, getting naked in his bathroom, getting ideas into her head that she shouldn't, had her very worried indeed.

CHAPTER EIGHT

GROWING UP AS a jack of all trades in Kings Cross, doing odd jobs for whoever would pay, had garnered Hudson a reputation for having sound business sense and good ideas.

Offering his shower to Mak hadn't been one of them.

What was it about this woman that brought out his latent knight-in-shining-armour complex in a big way?

It had been bad enough sitting through two hours of rehearsal. One hundred and twenty excruciating minutes of watching Mak gyrate and contort and flaunt her hot body encased in skin-tight cotton and Lycra.

Pure torture.

And this was only the first day. How the hell would he keep a grip on his lust and pretend having her back in his life as a friend was all he wanted?

His only saving grace was the tight turnaround on this project. Two weeks of rehearsals. Two weeks of nightly shows. Then Mak would move on to the next show, and he could breathe again. Because right now, with the thought of her naked behind his bathroom door, he couldn't. His lungs felt as if they'd been clogged with concrete. His cock, too.

'Idiot,' he muttered, kicking a heavy wooden leg of the coffee table. It didn't do much to relieve the frustration.

The bathroom door creaked open, and Hudson swore his heart stopped. If Mak came out here dressed in only a towel he'd have to make a run for it before he followed through on every single filthy fantasy running on repeat through his head.

'Uh, I hate to be a pain, but there's a problem with the flick mixer and I can't get the water temperature right.'

He risked a glance towards the bathroom and saw her poking her head around the barely opened door. Caught a glimpse of creamy bare shoulder. The hint of a towel lower.

Fuck. He'd forgotten to call the plumber this morning to fix the dodgy shower mixer. He'd had the same problem, unable to adjust the perfect temperature, and it had taken a lot of jiggling and fiddling to get it right earlier that day.

'Have you tried moving it around?'

She wrinkled her nose. 'I've tried everything. Do you think you could fix it for me? I really can't afford to be late to this costume fitting.'

'Sure,' he said, when he should've said 'hell no' and headed down to the club where the music would be so loud it could drown out his licentious thoughts. As if. 'But only if you're decent.'

He'd meant it as a joke but he caught the flare of

awareness in her eyes as he broached the distance between them. It didn't help.

Neither did the sight of her wrapped in one of his navy towels. It ended mid-thigh, exposing her long dancer legs, toned and tanned. Stunning. He couldn't help it: he looked his fill before letting his gaze drift upward to where she clutched a loose knot over her chest.

That was when he saw the telltale poke of nipples through the cotton. It wasn't cold in here, which meant Mak was as turned on as he was.

His cock gave a throb, as if to remind him he had a beautiful, half-naked woman in his bathroom and what the hell was he going to do about it.

The smart answer would be nothing.

But he'd given up being smart around the time he'd been dumb enough to drive this woman away first time around.

He took a step towards her. 'Mak, I—'

'Fix the shower, Hudson, please.' She held up one of her hands, letting the towel slip a little. Revealing a swell of breast that left him salivating.

'I'll fix it for you on one condition.'

Her eyes widened imperceptibly, her irises expanding. 'What?'

'You let me watch you.'

The dare tumbled from his lips and he didn't regret it. If he was to have any chance of convincing her he wanted her beyond friendship, he needed to see if he could get past that night five years ago that changed everything. Seeing her stripping on stage had brought up a host of awful memories he'd rather forget and he'd reacted accordingly. This time, he had to get past his hang-ups before he told her how much he wanted her and to do that, he had to see her naked.

Testing himself might be the stupidest thing he'd ever done but better to know now before he fucked up their tentatively re-established friendship because his libido couldn't be quelled.

Her lips parted on a shocked O. It wouldn't surprise him if she slapped him. He half expected it. Braced for it. Tension made his muscles bunch beneath his shirt.

He needed a workout after this; should hit the gym tonight, no matter what the time. He had a feeling he'd have a lot of tension to work off.

'The last time you saw me naked, it didn't work out so well,' she said, aiming for flippant, but he caught the worried undertone to her comment. Like she was testing him.

This time, he wouldn't be so foolish as to fail.

'Don't do that, try to trivialise something I did that screwed up our friendship,' he said, taking another step towards her. 'We've moved on from the past and this thing between us now? So frigging potent I can't see straight. You feel it too?'

He held his breath for an eternity, her indecision clear in the conflicted emotions flickering in her eyes, before her barely perceptible nod encouraged him to continue. 'I want you, Mak. No complications. No expectations. But I know you have to be somewhere so, for now, let me watch.'

It sounded so dirty when he said it out loud, but she

hadn't turfed him out yet. In fact, the longer she stared at him with a mix of fascination and wariness, he got the impression she wasn't so averse to his suggestion.

'Fix the mixer, fast,' she finally said, so soft and breathy he wasn't sure he'd heard right.

'So that's a yes?'

'Just fix the thing,' she said, releasing her grip on the towel.

It slithered to the floor. Along with his jaw.

She was breathtakingly beautiful, the kind of exquisite that made his chest ache.

The first time he'd seen her naked he'd been angry and resentful and out of his mind with worry. He hadn't wanted that life for her. He'd seen what it had done to his mum and it killed him deep inside every time he thought of what she'd done to make ends meet. For him.

Since that fateful night he'd deliberately blotted out the memory of Mak naked, hadn't wanted to taint his image of her.

Now, with her standing in front of him, uncertain yet unabashed, he looked his fill. Imprinting every single detail on his memory. Her perky C cups. Pale pink nipples. Mole above her belly button. Trimmed golden-red bush.

Perfection.

She snapped her fingers, breaking him out of his trance. 'The shower, remember?'

He managed a rueful grin and pointed to his head. 'Sorry. My little brain was caught up admiring the splendour of your beauty while my big brain,' he said, pointing lower, 'is telling me to strip naked too.'

'Don't you dare. I don't have time.' She waggled her finger at him, which would've held more sway as an admonishment if her breasts hadn't jiggled with the action too. 'Shower. Now.'

How he managed to fix the damn shower mixer he'd never know, considering his hands were as fumbling and clumsy as his efforts to not stare at her. Damn near impossible.

After four botched attempts, he had the water at a reasonable temperature and stepped back, allowing her to enter the double stall.

'Room for two in there,' he pointed out, clenching his hands into fists to stop from reaching for her as she stepped past him, smelling of sweat and arousal.

'Maybe some other time.' And with a jaunty flick of her hip, she closed the door in his face.

But didn't turn her back on him. Instead, she pumped body wash into her hand from his dispenser and slowly, leisurely ran it down the front of her body from neck to navel.

Damned if it wasn't the most erotic thing he'd ever seen.

The shower stall started steaming up and no way in hell would he tolerate his view being obliterated, so he flicked the exhaust switch and perched on the edge of the bath tub to enjoy the show.

He couldn't believe his luck. When he'd thrown out his challenge he'd expected Mak to verbally flay him, calling him anything from pervert to sicko.

Never in his wildest dreams had he expected to be privy to this.

Eyes closed. Water sluicing down her body. Her hands rubbing her breasts, over and under in hypnotic circles, lathering up so that bubbles covered her. Drifting lower to her stomach. Lower yet…

His breath caught as her fingers skirted her mound, before momentarily delving between the folds.

Lust pounded through his body in time with his heart. Every muscle tensed in his desperation to hold back. Every ounce of common sense swamped by how badly he wanted to touch her. Fuck, he was in blue ball hell watching her. Wanting her. Craving her with every horny cell in his body.

When she let out a low moan, Hudson couldn't take it any longer. He sprang up from the bathtub, wrenched open the shower door and knelt.

Her eyes flew open. 'What are you doing?'

'This.' He leaned forward and grasped her ass with his hands, edging her towards him.

'This wasn't part of the deal…ooh…'

He tongued her, a long, slow sweep between her slick folds that had her bracing against the shower walls and arching into his mouth ever so slightly.

It was all the encouragement he needed to devour her. Alternating between sucking and nibbling. Teasing her clit with repeated little flicks before returning to laving her deeper.

She went a little crazy. Hips undulating. Thrusting at him. Urging him on. Her incoherent pleadings escalated along with every lap of his tongue. So responsive. So fucking hot.

The moment before she came he slipped a finger inside her, another, pumping into her as he licked her. She fell apart, her knees buckling as she yelled, 'oh, yeah,' so loud his ears rang.

Smug that he'd satisfied her the way he wanted but calling on every ounce of restraint not to push her up against the shower stall and bury himself deep, he stood, water dripping down his face. That was nothing compared to his soaked clothes.

When he started to back away, her hand snaked out to capture his.

'Where do you think you're going?'

'To change.'

Confusion clouded her eyes and she gnawed on her bottom lip. 'But… I mean…what about you?'

Suddenly shy, she glanced away. 'Why don't you join me in here?'

It was the best invitation he'd heard all day—all frigging decade—but the first time they had sex he intended to make it count. All night long.

'I'd like nothing better but you've got an appointment, remember?'

Her muttered 'Fuck the appointment' made him smile as he closed the shower door.

'Trust me, babe, if I joined you, we wouldn't get out of there for a week, so how about you take that as a prelude and I'll do the right thing and wait for you out there?' He jerked a thumb towards the hallway.

She didn't respond, staring at him in wide-eyed wonder, as if she couldn't believe what had just happened.

Join the club.

Eventually, she nodded and turned away, but not before he saw something that made his heart soar.

The coy smile of a well-satisfied woman who wanted more.

CHAPTER NINE

'HEY, HONEY, I'M HOME,' Charlotte called out her standard greeting as she entered the lounge room of their tiny Bondi apartment, dumped her satchel and fell into the nearest seat. 'I hope you had a better day than I did.'

Makayla's day had been average. What had happened after rehearsal in Hudson's bathroom had more than made up for it.

Even now, three hours later, she couldn't believe it.

He'd gone down on her.

Giving her an orgasm to end all orgasms.

What that man could do with his tongue…

'Why was your day so bad?' Makayla managed a sensible question while inside she still screamed, *Oh, my God, Hudson and his tongue!*

'New boss from hell.' Charlotte took off her heels and stretched her legs out, scrunching her toes. 'Haven't even met him in person yet but taking orders from him remotely is bad enough.'

'I thought all accountants were perfectly polite

types who treated each other with dignity and respect?'

Charlotte flipped her the bird. 'That's how much I respect your opinion. As for my boss being an accountant, I think he's one of those business drones who only see the bottom line and couldn't give a flying fig about personnel.'

'Sounds like a rough day,' she said, busting to get Charlotte's opinion on what had gone down with Hudson—literally—but not sure she wanted to talk about it.

'Looks like yours wasn't.' Charlotte tucked her legs under her, eyeing her with curiosity. 'You've got this weird smug smirk thing happening.'

'Rehearsal went well,' she said, her lips twitching, unable to stop a grin spreading over her face, the kind of grin that made her cheeks ache. 'Really well.'

'What the…?' Charlotte's eyes narrowed before she squealed. 'No way. You slept with someone on your first day?'

'Of course not.' But she'd wanted to drag Hudson into the shower with her. She'd admired his self-control while cursing him for it.

When he'd first asked to watch, she'd been shocked at his cheekiness. He'd asked her to do the very thing that had ensured he'd ended their friendship five years earlier.

Yet her surprise at his audacity had quickly given way to intrigue and she'd been turned on by the suggestion. But she'd wanted to make him sweat. In trying to prove a point—that he was duplicitous for wanting to watch her naked when he'd freaked that one time she'd done it with good reason—her plan had backfired.

Having him watch her shower had been the most erotic thing she'd ever experienced. She'd tried to stick with the programme of deliberate torture as revenge for how badly he'd treated her the last time he'd seen her naked, intent on purposely driving him crazy. Unfortunately she'd driven herself nuts in the process.

She'd never been so turned on, had been shocked yet relieved when he'd opened that shower door. Not that she was a complete fool. She'd known what might happen when she'd agreed to let him watch her. Had counted on it, so she could call him out for being a hypocrite and release all the pent-up regret that she'd harboured despite their newly awakened friendship now. She'd planned on stopping him with a few terse words. She hadn't expected to admire him because he'd been man enough to acknowledge the attraction simmering between them.

Even as her resistance had crumbled and her residual anger had faded, she'd had reservations. Getting physical with Hudson would change everything. He'd already seen her naked and found her lacking once. What was to say his freak-out that night years ago wouldn't happen again because of his baggage she didn't know about?

She'd been an idiot. She should've known that in agreeing to his challenge out of anger, it would backfire on her. She'd been curious to see how far she could push him. She hadn't expected him to push back…and how. But she couldn't get past one question that kept bugging her: was he genuinely so damn hot for her that he couldn't resist or had he been trying to prove a point—to himself—as she'd been doing?

Whatever his rationale, when her anger had dwindled and she'd released the bitterness of the past, she'd realised Hudson was staring at her with admiration, not disgust, and she'd never felt so empowered as she'd showered in front of him. Knowing he was finally looking at her the way she wanted him to look. Knowing he wanted her.

'You so did sleep with someone. Look at your cheeks!' Charlotte yelled. 'You're crimson.'

Makayla pressed her palms to her scorching cheeks. 'I didn't sleep with anyone but there may have been other stuff going on.'

'Ooh, do tell.' Charlotte rubbed her hands together, but before Makayla could reveal the partial truth, the doorbell rang.

'That'll be Abby,' she said, glancing at her watch. 'She's bringing leftovers from the patisserie.'

'Good, I'm starved.' Charlotte leapt nimbly to her feet, her petite frame always making Makayla feel like an ogre. 'Dealing with an asshole boss gives me an appetite.'

Dealing with Makayla's boss gave her an appetite too, but not for food.

'Hi, lovelies.' Abby breezed into the room brandishing the distinct pink and gold cardboard bags from Le Miel. 'I come bearing gifts.'

'Whatever you're offering, I'll have three of each,'

Charlotte said, padding into the kitchen to get plates. 'Chardonnay okay for you two?'

'Please,' Abby said, shooting Makayla a 'what's up?' look when she hadn't said anything.

'Tell you in a minute,' Makayla said, waiting until Charlotte had poured them each a glass of wine and their plates were covered with lemon tartlets, petite croissants and *beignets*.

'Makayla's been up to no good with someone at work,' Charlotte said, popping a tartlet into her mouth whole. 'And she's about to spare this poor, pathetic spinster no details.'

'Someone at work?' Predictably, Abby's ears all but twitched. 'Tell me it's Hudson. He's gorgeous.' She swivelled towards Charlotte and wiggled her eyebrows. 'You know the actor Tom Hiddleston?'

Charlotte's forehead crinkled before she snapped her fingers. 'English, right? Tall, blond, blue eyes, incredibly hot?'

Abby nodded. 'Hudson could be his twin.'

Charlotte wolf whistled. 'But isn't he your boss?'

Makayla sighed, knowing she should've remembered that salient point around the time he'd opened that shower door. 'Technically, yes, but we're old friends.'

'Friends or *friends*?' Charlotte made smoochy sounds. 'I do love a good juicy friends-to-lovers saga.'

Makayla snorted and pointed to a towering stack of novels on a side table. 'Stick to your romance novels because there's not much to tell.'

Abby's grin channelled pure evil. 'Maybe I should ask Tanner—'

'Don't you dare.' Makayla glared at Abby, who feigned innocence before taking a bite out of one of her signature croissants.

Makayla loved Abby's pastries but if she ate half of what Abby did she wouldn't be able to fit into her leotards, let alone dance.

'You'll have to give us something, my friend, otherwise I'm getting Tanner to do some digging.' Abby dusted off her hands and reached for her wine glass. 'And trust me, he's more of a gossip than I am.'

'Okay, okay, sheesh.' Makayla blew out a breath, keen to get her friends' take on what had gone down with Hudson—literally—but nervous they'd reiterate what she already knew. She was stupid for complicating a working relationship with her boss. 'But you promise not to breathe a word of this to Tanner, okay?'

Abby hesitated before nodding. 'We tell each other everything, but considering you're my best friend and Hudson's his, we'll stay out of it.'

Makayla glanced at Charlotte, who held up her hands. 'Hey, who would I tell? You two are the only friends I have.'

Makayla searched for the right words, something to tell her friends that didn't involve revealing everything. Before realising if she left out the juicy stuff there wouldn't be much to tell.

'The short version? I had a dress fitting tonight for another show I'm doing, a one-off. Rehearsals ran late so I wouldn't have had time to get back here to shower. Hudson lives in an apartment over Embue so he offered me his shower to save time.' Makayla felt heat flush her cheeks as Abby's eyes widened to saucer proportion.

'You didn't! He showered with you?'

Charlotte blew a raspberry. 'I'm so freaking jealous. You lead the most exciting life ever.'

Not usually. Exciting things didn't happen to Makayla often. Today had been an aberration…that she'd remember for a very long time. 'Do you want to hear the rest or not?'

'Yes!' both girls yelled in unison, so she continued. 'The shower mixer thingy wasn't working and I couldn't get the water temp right. So I called out to him to fix it.'

'And?' Charlotte prompted, her elbows resting on her knees, chin in her hands, leaning forward and hanging on her every word.

'He said he'd fix it.' Makayla paused for dramatic effect. 'If I let him watch me shower.'

Charlotte squealed and Abby's mouth dropped open. 'No way. That's so hot.'

'I know, right?' Makayla's skin pebbled at the remembrance of having Hudson watch her with that intense gaze of his. Like he couldn't look away. Like he was really seeing her for the first time. 'I should never have agreed but we've got this attraction going on, always have, so I thought why not?'

'Why not indeed?' Charlotte sighed and slumped back on the sofa, wistfulness clouding her eyes. 'You are so lucky.'

Since they'd been flatmates, Makayla had never seen Charlotte date, let alone have a boyfriend. She'd tried to encourage her to go clubbing or go out for drinks at their local bar on a Friday night, but Charlotte preferred reading to socialising. She hoped she could drag her to Embue to watch her perform. If Makayla was in a man slump, Charlotte was in severe drought.

'So what happened after that?' Abby prompted.

'I was angry at first, really mad.' For reasons she wouldn't go into with her friends. She'd left the past behind and had no intention of rehashing it. 'I wanted to tell him to stick his ludicrous challenge.' Her grin turned sly. 'But then I wanted to make him sweat for being so audacious, so while he watched I may have played up to him a tad and…he, uh…ended up in the shower…' Hell, there was no easy way to say this, so she blurted, 'He went down on me.'

'Hells bells.' Charlotte almost fell off her chair she leaned forward so far, while Abby tut-tutted. 'Bad girl.'

'Or good, very, very good, depending how you look at it.' Makayla couldn't keep the smug grin off her face now she'd come to terms with her fall from grace. And she'd fallen far. From indignant woman scorned to moaning, wanton goddess, she'd given in to Hudson when she should've rallied against his injustice. But the moment he'd lapped at her with his tongue her outrage at his double standards had been obliterated and, considering the ferocity of her orgasm, she couldn't be sorry for that. 'Let's just say if I hadn't had to rush off I'd probably still be there, returning the favour.'

'You two are so going to end up together,' Charlotte said, sounding pensive. 'I can sense it.'

Abby, the more practical of her friends, seemed less caught up in the romanticism. 'What does he think about this fling?'

Something in Makayla's chest tightened at Abby's casual labelling of what she'd shared with Hudson as a fling. She shouldn't care, because if things proceeded with them that was exactly what it would be.

But having Abby articulate it meant her friend either thought she wasn't up for anything more or she knew more about Hudson via Tanner and he wasn't.

'We didn't really get to talk,' Makayla said, some of her earlier enthusiasm at getting the girls' opinions dwindling. 'But I like him. He likes me. The shower thing could be a prelude to more.'

'Do you want that?'

'Of course she does,' Charlotte answered for her. 'If this guy is as hot as you say, why wouldn't she?'

Abby's furtive glance away made Makayla's heart sink. 'What aren't you telling me, Abs?'

Abby hesitated before giving a brief nod. 'Tanner and Hudson have been mates since high school. According to Tanner, Hudson hasn't been in a relationship ever. He dates a few times max, moves on. Are you okay with that, considering you share a past?'

Makayla's heart foolishly lifted at the thought of Hudson never being involved with a woman long term. Not that she was interested in changing his track record—far from it—but it meant that if they did have a fling it wouldn't change the status quo for either of them.

She didn't have time for mess. Not when this job could be the first step to achieving her dream.

'We both grew up in Kings Cross. Our paths crossed regularly and we ended up friends. Then we had a falling out and we weren't any more. But all that's in the past, and whatever happens now we'll both know where we stand.'

Sounded nice in theory but Makayla knew it had the potential to be way more complicated than that.

Working with Hudson could provide her with contacts she needed to climb the industry ladder. It could lead to her big break. So what happened if they had a fling but it soured? Their friendship had gone south once before and she still didn't know the real reason behind his outburst that had effectively ended them. This time, it could have far more severe consequences.

The concern creasing Abby's brow faded. 'As long as you both know the score before you start something up, you'll be fine.'

'I think they've already started something up,' Charlotte said with a cheeky wink. 'You should go for it, sweetie. Have some fun. You deserve it.'

'Here's to both of you getting clean in many showers together.' Abby raised her glass in a toast. 'Or should that be getting dirty?'

Makayla chuckled and clinked glasses with the girls. While she didn't need their approval to take things further with Hudson, it had been helpful to use them as sounding boards.

Not that she had a hope in hell of backing out. She'd

made her decision the second she'd let the towel drop and allowed Hudson to see her naked several hours ago.

A bold move or a moment of madness?

Guess she'd soon find out.

CHAPTER TEN

WORK HAD KICKED Hudson's ass tonight.

Patrons flocked to Embue for a good time on a daily basis but some nights were crazy busy. Being the manager for Sydney's hottest nightclub had its advantages. He counted the coolest celebrities and sports stars as friends, knew every up-and-comer in the city and had his pick of gorgeous women.

He should've been rapt that Australia's biggest beauty pageant contingent had chosen Embue as their venue for an after-party tonight. Instead, as he watched countless stunning women swan by him wearing next to nothing, sporting bodies that could make a guy grovel, all he could think about was Makayla.

Was she regretting their earlier encounter?

Was she looking forward to the next?

Was she thinking about him at all?

He sure as hell couldn't stop thinking about her.

He'd never expected to take things so far. He'd wanted to test himself, to see if he'd moved on from the past, to ensure that seeing her naked again wouldn't resurrect the old feelings of repugnance; not against her, but for what seeing her naked the first time represented to him.

Thankfully, nothing but desire had filled him, pounding through his blood to a relentless beat he couldn't ignore. He'd never been prone to impulsiveness but watching her soap and stroke herself had lit something within he couldn't deny.

He had to prove—to both of them—that he saw her as a beautiful, desirable woman. That he'd left his reservations from the past behind. That he'd moved on, for both their sakes.

When he'd opened the shower stall, he'd had no idea what to do. Kiss her maybe. Touch her. But the look in her eyes had slayed him: as if she half expected his rejection all over again.

That realisation had gutted him and he'd known he had to give her pleasure and keep a tight rein on his.

Tasting her, hearing her tiny mewls of satisfaction, had been amazing. But he couldn't forget that damn look in her eyes and the fact he'd put it there with his appalling treatment of her five years earlier.

Scowling, he made his umpteenth round of the club, doing impromptu spot checks on everything from the cleanliness of the cocktail glasses to dance-floor spills. Staff must've sensed his mood because they steered clear, ensuring their workstations were spotless, not giving him the usual grief.

His cell buzzed in his pocket and he fished it out, his heart giving a traitorous leap when Mak's name flashed up on the screen.

She'd sent him a text. Short and sweet.

I've got 2 tix for show @ Opera House 2moro nite. U free?

He worked nights, but if Mak wanted to spend any time with him after what had happened earlier, it meant she didn't want to castrate him for his boldness and was open to more.

Nothing could keep him away.

Spying Tanner near the sound booth, he crossed the club with determined strides, eager to give her an answer before she changed her mind or asked someone else to accompany her.

'Hey, bozo, what are you putting in the drinks?' Tanner gestured around. 'This place is packed tonight.'

'Word travels. That, and you've got the best manager in the business.'

'Modest, much?' Tanner leaned against the console, his white T-shirt fluorescent in the club lights. 'What's up?'

'Speaking of being the best manager in the business, can I have tomorrow night off?'

Tanner's eyebrows rose. 'You never ask for time off. What gives?'

'A show at the Opera House I want to check out.'

'Uh-huh.' Tanner tapped his temple, pretending to think. 'Is this technically work? You checking out a show to get ideas for the show here?'

Hudson didn't lie to his best friend. But he knew if he told the truth, he'd never hear the end of it.

'Something like that,' he said, the half-truth lodging in his throat.

'Sure, go ahead. Knock yourself out.' Tanner shrugged. 'Say hi to Mak for me.'

'What?'

Tanner guffawed and slapped him on the back. 'Listen, dickhead, when a workaholic like you asks for a night off for the first time in five years it must involve a woman. And seeing as Mak had you in a spin after the audition, it has to be her. Correct?'

'You're full of shit,' Hudson said, glad his friend knew him so well. 'She has a spare ticket, she asked me to go, that's it.'

'Keep telling yourself that,' Tanner said, grinning like a doofus. 'Though you've heard the saying, right? Don't screw the crew?'

'Like you did with Abby?'

'*Touché*, my smitten friend.' Tanner shrugged. 'Don't say I didn't warn you.'

Hudson flipped him the bird and stalked off, already tapping a response to Mak.

He didn't need any warnings. He already knew that getting involved with Mak could lead to disaster.

But with relentless desire pounding through his body, making him want her with a mindless intensity he couldn't shake no matter how hard he tried, he knew that some things were worth the risk.

CHAPTER ELEVEN

HUDSON HAD OFFERED to pick Makayla up but she'd cited a late shift at the patisserie and arranged to meet him on the steps of the Opera House instead.

Pathetic, considering she'd invited him. No use chickening out now. But that was exactly what she'd done, ever since Charlotte had presented her with the tickets last night after their gossip session.

At the time, she'd justified her decision to invite him as a way to thank him for the job opportunity. Now, twenty-four hours later, with the prospect of sitting next to him in the dark, trying to keep her mind on the recital and not on the delectable guy making her think naughty thoughts, her decision didn't seem so smart.

In reality, she could dress up her invitation any way she liked but the truth was she wanted to spend more time with him.

He'd been out of her life for years and in less than a week, he'd insinuated his way back into it without trying.

She couldn't stop thinking about him.

Probably her hormones wanting a repeat of what went down in his shower too, but she owed it to herself to explore this thing they had between them.

She'd been dating regularly for years. Not without any thought for the future, but for the simple pleasure of having fun. She hadn't slept with a lot of guys—she was too picky for that—but she liked dating, enjoyed sex, and hadn't had enough of either over the last year.

Time to rectify that with a guy she actually respected and admired.

Hudson had always been larger than life for her. The kind of guy who strode into a room and everyone took notice. Back then, he'd been amenable and pleasant and a hard worker, friendly to everyone. His *laissez faire* attitude had got him regular work around the Cross, because no one doubted if they hired Hudson their work would get done.

Despite his busy schedule, he'd always had time for her. Had listened to her wax lyrical about everything, from her favourite boy band to her crappiest teacher. She'd never mentioned any crushes, because he'd been it for her.

Here they were, five years later, with her crush stalking towards her, looking incredible in black trousers, black shirt and dark grey sports jacket. Perfectly tailored designer clothes that accentuated the lean hardness of his body. A body she'd be seeing naked by the end of tonight if she had her way.

'Glad you could make it,' she said when he reached her and leaned down to brush a kiss on her cheek.

'Wouldn't miss it.' He straightened, but his aftershave lingered, a heady mix of crisp citrus and deeper exotic undertones. Mysterious. Alluring. Scrumptious.

'I didn't know you're that into opera?'

'I'm not.' His enigmatic stare left her in little doubt what he was really into. 'But I'd be a fool to pass up the opportunity to spend an evening with you.'

'Smooth talker.' She smiled and gave him a gentle nudge with her elbow. 'Shall we go in?'

'Sure.'

She forced her body to relax when he placed a hand in the small of her back, an innocuous gesture to guide her. But she couldn't stop her nerve endings from going haywire, firing and zapping and making her want to ditch the opera in favour of the nearest hotel room.

'I love this place,' he said as they stepped inside the iconic Opera House, the soaring ceilings inside as beautiful as the white sails outside.

'Have you been to many shows here?'

He nodded, glancing around with an interest bordering on reverence. 'The theatre company I'm involved with attends shows regularly here so I tag along whenever I can.'

'I'd never have picked you to have an interest in theatre,' she said, wondering how many other things she didn't know about him.

It had been five long years since they'd last spoken and it struck her anew. What did she really know about Hudson Watt?

Back then, she'd known he favoured orange juice over pineapple, preferred Aussie Rules football over rugby and liked jazz over pop. Now, she knew next to nothing about him and it saddened her.

What would their relationship be like now if they'd stayed in touch?

'I guess working around the Cross clubs all those years, seeing the dance shows, rubbed off on me.' His tone was curt, clipped, and she knew why.

He didn't want to talk about some of the club shows at the Cross. Not when some of them involved stripping, the reason they'd fallen out in the first place. But if she wanted to know more about him, she couldn't back down, even when the going got tough.

'So you're interested in the production side of things?'

He nodded, his shoulders still rigid with tension. 'I've done a lot of behind-the-scenes stuff in the theatre company. Got me thinking what it would be like to combine the show side of things with clubbing.' He shrugged. 'I put together a proposal, Tanner gave me a chance.'

'So that means I need to dance my ass off so you can impress your boss to do more shows?'

'Something like that,' he said, his mouth curving into a slow smile. 'But please look after that ass. I happen to like it.'

Her pulse leapt, but she managed a demure, 'I'll bear that in mind.'

'You do that.' They'd reached their seats, and he waited until they'd sat before leaning across to murmur in her ear, 'Because if you need any assistance looking after it, I'm your man.'

She turned towards him and their eyes met. Even in the dim lighting she could see the spark, the lust, the heat. It gave her courage to reach across and rest her hand on his thigh. Low enough to be decent. High enough to be suggestive.

'You'll kill my concentration if you do that.'

In response, she slid a little higher and squeezed.

'I never did like opera all that much anyway,' he said, covering her hand with his, waiting until the lights went out before guiding it higher.

Yowza. He was big. Hard. Her fingers curled around him a little and she heard a muffled groan.

Makayla had no idea how they lasted through the first act: forty-five long excruciating minutes of exquisite costumes and pitch-perfect singing. Usually, she would've been enthralled. Instead, all she could focus on was how Hudson felt beneath her hand. How he could hold himself perfectly still, not moving a muscle, yet his rigidity conveying a restraint that left her awestruck.

As the falsetto strains of the lead vocalist faded and the lights flickered on, Hudson released her hand and she straightened, blinking at him as her eyes adjusted.

'What do you fancy for intermission?'

She couldn't imagine sipping champagne, making small talk and sitting through a torturous second act, wanting him more with every passing minute.

So she looked him in the eye and said, 'You.'

CHAPTER TWELVE

HUDSON DIDN'T CARE about speeding fines at this time of night. He happily broke the land speed record between Circular Quay and his apartment. Besides, he couldn't have driven slowly if he'd tried. Not with Mak sitting next to him, radiating a barely restrained energy that had the air between them almost crackling.

He'd felt it the moment he'd greeted her on the Opera House steps. As if something had shifted between them. Something minute and indescribable but there all the same, pulling them together, as if it were inevitable.

He'd been determined to fight it because he viewed her invitation to attend the opera with her as a huge step between them. An unspoken acknowledgement on her behalf that she'd forgiven him and they might have something more than friendship between them.

So he'd made small talk. Planned on sitting through the entire performance before suggesting they head back to his place for a drink.

Never in his wildest dreams had he anticipated Mak

wanting to leave halfway through the opera because she couldn't keep her hands off him.

When she'd touched him…did she have any idea what she did to him? He'd been rock-hard for forty-five goddamn minutes and he could've shouted for joy when she'd wanted to leave.

As he pulled into his car spot in the underground car park and killed the engine, he knew they were on the cusp of a massive shift in their relationship.

The point of no return.

So being an idiotic gentleman to the end, he gave her a last chance to back out.

'You sure about this?' He stared out of the windshield, unable to look at her. If he did, he knew he wouldn't be able to resist hauling her into his arms and that would take the decision out of her hands completely.

'Never been surer.'

She didn't touch him. She didn't need to. The conviction in her tone brooked no argument.

She wanted this as much as he did.

Which meant he couldn't get her upstairs fast enough.

She'd stepped out of the car before he had a chance to open her door, so he offered her his hand.

She took it and didn't let go until they were inside his apartment, the door barely closing before she was on him. Pushing him against the nearest wall. Slamming her body against his. Reaching for his zipper.

The thing with quick gratification, it could be incredibly hot but was over too fast. For his first time with the woman who'd featured in his fantasies for years he wanted to take things slow. Real slow.

'Hey, I want you,' he said, holding her arms and easing her back a fraction. 'I've wanted you for ever. So let me savour every single moment of this.'

The corners of her lush mouth kicked up in a devilish smile. 'So you want to torture me?'

'Call it building anticipation rather than torture.' He relaxed his grip on her arms and started sliding his palms up and down her bare skin, feeling it pebble beneath his touch. 'Quite frankly, you drive me crazy and I want to be buried inside you in two seconds flat.'

'Way too fast,' she said, her glance coy from beneath lowered lashes. 'But considering you sat through that entire first act rock-hard, how slow exactly do you want to take this?'

She pressed her pelvis against him. 'Because, honey, there's a difference between building anticipation and killing me slowly.'

He laughed, loving her honesty, loving that they could talk like this. They'd always been open with each other, had trusted each other. Until it had all imploded.

But he couldn't think about that night. Couldn't think about the secrets she probably harboured. Secrets that could drive him to distraction and wreck this before they'd even begun, if he was stupid enough to let them.

He had Mak in his arms.

Wanting him.

Mak.

No way in hell would he let the past or any doubts derail what promised to be the best night of his life.

'Dance with me,' he said, smiling when her eyebrows rose in surprise. 'Ever since I saw you audition for me, I imagined what it would be like having your incredible body moving close to mine.'

'Vertical sex, huh?' She pretended to ponder a moment, before nodding. 'I like it.'

He would too, as he led her by the hand to his stereo system, did a quick scroll through a smooth playlist, and chose one of his favourite classic songs.

'Prince? Seriously?' She slapped him playfully on the arm. 'Exactly how old are you?'

'Old enough to know better, old enough to not give a damn and do the bad stuff regardless.'

As the first sultry beats filled the air, he took her other hand, his body pulsing with barely controlled desire for her. Then she started moving in time to the music and all he could do for a moment was stare.

She had an inherent elegance that transformed into unadulterated heat as she danced. Her body took on a life of its own, as if the bass were a part of her. Sinuous writhing combined with sensuous hip rolls. Languid shoulder shimmies alternating with some seriously hot ass wiggling.

He was a goner.

He tugged on her hands, hard, intent on devouring her. But she resisted, her sexy smile ratcheting up the sizzle between them.

'I thought you wanted to prolong this?'

'I lied,' he muttered, his plans to take things slow

shot to hell the second she wiggled her ass at him. 'Sitting through that opera was foreplay enough and my self-control is shot to shit with you putting the moves on me.'

She quirked an eyebrow, her faux innocence not fooling him for a second. 'I'm merely dancing, just like you wanted to.'

'Don't listen to me. I'm an idiot.'

She chuckled and took a step closer. Close enough he could smell her, sweat mingling with her sultry fragrance, a heady combination that drove him wild.

'But you didn't dance?'

'You danced enough for the both of us,' he said, palming her ass and pulling her close. 'God, you drive me wild.'

Her slow, seductive smile made his heart pound. 'Show me.'

He didn't have to be asked twice. 'You look sensational in this dress but I've been wanting to get you out of it since the moment I saw you tonight.'

The simple black halter that ended below her knees screamed understated class, but the silky fabric that clung to her body in all the right places ensured it transformed the dress from demure to sexy as hell.

'Be my guest.' She turned around, giving him an unimpeded view of smooth skin. No tan lines. Interesting.

Thankfully, she'd tied a simple knot at her neck and he had it undone with a flick of his wrist. The material slithered down her front, and he bit back a groan as his fingertips skated down her spine to her waist.

He toyed with the zipper for a moment, his throbbing cock urging him to rip the damn thing and be done with it. But there had to be something to delayed gratification so he slid it down slowly.

Revealing a black satin thong.

Hot damn.

The dress fell to the floor in a whisper of silk, leaving her standing before him in stilettos and that thong.

Her ass was as sweet as he'd imagined, rounded yet taut. A good handful. He palmed it. Kneading it. Her low groan better than any aphrodisiac.

'Turn around,' he said, his order a growl.

He stepped back as she did so, allowing himself to look his fill.

Exquisite.

The first time he'd seen her naked, he'd allowed himself one illicit glance before looking away, incensed. In his shower, he'd been too gobsmacked to stare too long.

This time, he intended to take his time.

Her breasts were perfect. Perky, full. With pretty pale pink nipples that stood to attention, begging to be sucked.

He glanced lower, zeroing in on where he wanted to be. Saw her hook her thumbs under the elastic of the thong. Push it down. Revealing heaven. Golden red, a deeper shade than her hair cascading around her shoulders.

In his shower, he'd devoured her too quickly. Had been hell-bent on giving her pleasure and giving in to the fantasy of tasting her. Tonight, he'd make sure he took his time.

Later.

She kicked away the thong and kinked a hip in a purely provocative pose. 'Shoes on or off?'

'You won't have time to take them off,' he said, launching himself at her.

But she stepped back and held him off with a hand on his chest. 'Uh-uh. One of us is way overdressed.'

'I don't need to undress.' He unzipped his fly, where his cock strained against the briefs beneath. 'There. Done.'

'You're not the only one who gets off by looking.' She gave him a little shove. 'I want to see you naked. Now.'

'Bossy,' he muttered, grinning as he shrugged out of his jacket and flung it away.

'Faster,' she said, sounding breathless.

So he obliged by popping buttons quickly and letting his shirt fall to the floor.

She made an appreciative sound deep in her throat as he unsnapped his trousers and stepped out of them. With her gaze riveted to his groin, he pushed down his jocks and almost crowed with pride as her jaw dropped.

'You felt big but…wow,' she said, sounding awed. 'This is going to be one hell of a night.'

He bit back his first response, 'Just one night?'

Because if that was all Mak was willing to give, he'd take it. No questions asked. He'd waited too long, wanted her too much, to spoil tonight with awkward conversations.

'Don't move,' she said, and stepped forward before kneeling at his feet.

'Mak, I want—fuck…' he groaned as she wrapped her mouth around him. Taking the tip of his cock between her lips. Flicking her tongue out to tease him. Licking him like she couldn't get enough. Driving him frigging nuts.

He watched her take him in deeper, the moist heat of her mouth making him grit his teeth. What she couldn't take into her mouth she wrapped her hand around and that was when the fun really began.

She started moving her hand and mouth in sync, sucking and licking as if he were all her favourite ice cream flavours rolled into one.

The hottest fucking thing he'd ever experienced.

But the pressure in his balls built too quickly so he had to stop. The first time he came he wanted to be inside her.

'Baby…' He laid a hand on her head and eased her away. She glanced up at him, questioning, and he knelt, bringing him to eye level. 'As much as I'm in blow-job heaven, I need to be inside you.'

'Okay,' she said, her lips curving in a saucy smile. 'Heaven, huh?'

'You have no idea.'

Then finally, after waiting forever to do this, he kissed her. Slow grazes of his lips against hers. Increasing the pressure each time. Lingering longer. Until her tongue darted out to touch his and he was lost.

Their tongues tangled as he hauled her against him, her breasts crushing against his chest, her skin soft beneath his touch but incredibly hot, as if she were burning up from the inside out.

He knew the feeling.

Breaking the kiss long enough to fish a condom out of his trouser pocket, he sheathed himself and returned to where he wanted to be. In Mak's arms.

'Lean back,' she said, pushing him slightly, until his back rested against the couch.

She straddled him, arms braced either side of his head. He held his breath as she lowered herself, her entrance nudging his cock.

Without breaking eye contact, she slid lower. Inch by exquisite inch. Her mouth open, eyes glazed, until she'd taken all of him inside her slick heat.

'You make me feel…wanton,' she said, raising her arms to lift the hair off her shoulders, tilting her head back, thrusting her breasts at him in a pose of sheer abandonment.

He thrust upward, garnering a smug smile from her, so he did it again. Holding her hips. Pushing upward. Savouring her moans, her pants.

She undulated on him, rising and falling in perfect synchronicity with the pounding in his head reverberating all the way down his spine to his balls.

He wanted to suck her nipples but he couldn't take his eyes off her, the way she rode him with wicked intent.

It was too much, too soon, but he had as much chance of not coming as he did of forgetting this incredible night. So he reached between them, circled her clit with his thumb. Felt the first ripples of her orgasm deep within.

She picked up the pace, sliding up and down with abandon, the sheen of sweat making her body glow. Unable to hold back a second longer, his body tensed and he gave one last flick against her clit, savouring the moment she fell apart. Her body stiff, breasts thrust upward, expression cataclysmic as she screamed his name and he came so hard he saw spots.

She slumped against him, clung to him and he held her tight.

There were no words.

Superfluous, considering what had just happened.

Mak had blown apart his world as he knew it.

CHAPTER THIRTEEN

MAKAYLA KNEW SHE should've left the moment her heart rate had returned to normal the first time they'd had sex in Hudson's living room.

But she'd been too sated, too languid to move, so she hadn't protested when he'd swept her up in his arms like some goddamn hero out of those romance novels Charlotte devoured and taken her to his bedroom.

Where she'd stayed all night.

Makayla never slept over with any of the guys she dated. She enjoyed the foreplay, tried to enjoy the sex, then left.

That was another thing. The sex. Usually, she got off more on the foreplay. The teasing. The flirting. The touches. The glances. The act itself, not so much. In her experience, most men didn't pay enough attention to her body beyond sticking it in and giving her orgasm a passing thought.

Not Hudson. Hudson had strummed her body like a maestro. Caressing every inch. Exploring every crevice with his mouth, his hands. Licking every erogenous zone. Coming back for more. Four times.

She'd never had sex five times in one night. Incredible. Memorable.

Diabolical.

Because as the first fingers of dawn stole through the blinds, highlighting the slumbering sex god by her side, all she could think was where the hell did they go from here?

'I can hear you thinking.' A low rumble came from beneath the covers as he rolled over to face her. 'Stop overanalysing.'

She tugged the sheet higher, feeling oddly vulnerable despite the many ways he'd already seen her body last night. 'Hey, I just woke up. I'm not overanalysing anything.'

'Sure you are,' he said, trailing a fingertip down her cheek in a tender gesture that brought an unexpected lump to her throat. 'To be expected after the way you ravaged me last night.'

She feigned mock outrage and swatted his hand away. 'As I recall, you did most of the ravaging, mister.'

'I remember.' His eyes darkened to indigo, the spark of lust unmistakeable. 'And I plan to do it all over again, starting now.'

Makayla would like nothing better than to lose herself under his skilful ministrations but she knew walking away without clarifying what had happened between them would be wrong considering she'd be seeing him at rehearsals this afternoon.

'Wait,' she said, placing a palm against his chest. His heart pounded beneath it. Strong. Steady. Dependable.

Just like Hudson. He'd been her rock growing up.

Her friend. Until he'd misjudged her and ended up leaving her alone like everyone else in her life.

She'd learned a hard lesson then: never depend on anyone but herself. A mantra she'd stuck to. It had served her well. Independence above all else.

But there was a fine line between independence and foolishness. And that was a line she'd be treading if she didn't acknowledge that thanks to Hudson she now had a shot at a serious career boost, but she might have screwed it up by sleeping with her boss.

'What's wrong?' A frown marred his brow and she itched to reach out and smooth it away.

'Don't get me wrong, last night was amazing, but…' She floundered, searching for the right words to convey her confusion and concern.

'But you don't want a repeat, is that it?' His frown deepened, his mouth twisting with regret.

'I… I don't know what I want,' she admitted, rubbing her neck to ease the tension making her muscles bunch. 'The sex we had was phenomenal and so damn rare I want to do it over and over again. But I've worked my ass off as a dancer for years and your show is the first big break I've had in ages, so I don't want to mess with that. Plus you're my boss and I don't want rumours circulating that I score roles by sleeping with the boss. So even if we do keep this thing between us going, it'll have to be a secret, but that sounds so dirty, and that's not us—'

'Whoa, slow down, take a breath.' He rested his hand on her waist, the heat comforting through the cotton. 'So the sex was phenomenal, huh?'

She huffed out an angry breath. 'Typical guy, homing in on the sex and ignoring the rest.'

'I'm kidding, sweetheart.' He leaned forward to brush a soft kiss against her lips. 'Are you saying you want us to continue this?'

She wanted to lie. She wanted to run, far from his persuasive mouth and soul-searching eyes. But this was Hudson, the guy who'd once looked out for her, and she wouldn't mess with their friendship again. Not when having him back in her life now was like a precious gift she'd unwrapped and savoured.

'At the risk of sounding like a complete idiot, I had a crush on you way back when, so last night was pretty damn incredible,' she said, relieved when his frown cleared. 'And yeah, call me greedy, I want more.'

A slow grin eased across his face. 'I'm all for more—'

'But I don't want it at the expense of my career.' She sounded callous, calculating, but it had to be this way. Self-preservation was the only thing that had kept her going all these years when she'd scrimped to get by. 'Call me heartless, whatever, but I've never let a relationship come between me and my goals and I'm not about to start now, even for you.'

'Wow,' he said, wariness creeping into his eyes. 'You're a straight shooter.'

'I have a low tolerance for BS.' She shrugged. 'So I guess we play this my way or not at all.'

'I have a low tolerance for ultimatums,' he said, his frown returning. 'But I get where you're coming from.'

An ache filled her chest and spread outward, numbing her arms. In telling him the truth, had she lost him before this had really begun?

'Where do we go from here?'

He took an eternity to answer, conflicting emotions scudding across his steady gaze. Hope. Concern. Excitement. Recalcitrance.

When he opened his mouth to respond, she braced for an answer she wouldn't like.

'Mak, I've fantasised about you for years and now that I've had one stupendous night with you, do you honestly think I'm stupid enough to let you go?' His hand resting on her waist drifted upward in a slow caress that ended at her face, where he cupped her cheek. 'We'll play this your way. Whatever you want. Whenever you want. No one needs to know but us.'

Relief made her tremble, and she launched herself at him, burying her face against his chest. 'Thank you.'

His arms slid around her, warm, comforting. She snuggled deeper, feeling like she'd just won the lottery, a great job and a sensational guy as a bonus. It had been a long time since luck had been on her side. She didn't want anything to mess this up.

'Mak?'

'Hmm?'

'If this is our secret, can we get to the dirty part now?'

She chuckled against his chest before easing away, feeling more light-hearted than she had in ages. 'I need to get to work.'

'This won't take long.'

His wolfish grin made her tingle with anticipation as he slid a condom on and scooted down the bed, taking the cover sheet with him. Leaving her bare and exposed, the faint red marks on her skin evidence of their wonderful night of debauchery.

He slid a finger between her folds, a long sweep that had her arching towards him. 'So wet,' he said, lifting the finger to his mouth before licking it. 'So sweet.'

Makayla stared at the most erotic thing she'd ever seen, him tasting her unashamedly. She loved how uninhibited he was, as if the sex was merely an extension of their friendship.

'What are you going to do—? *Ooh...*' He nudged her knees apart, positioned himself and drove into her in one smooth thrust.

'No time for foreplay, you said.' He lifted her ass with his hands and slid a pillow under it, lifting her hips, giving him better access to hit her sweet spot when he thrust again. 'So I better make this quickie count.'

In response, Makayla wrapped her legs around him and interlocked her ankles, while bracing her hands behind her head. 'Go right ahead.'

He laughed at her devil-may-care posture and reached down to rub her clit. 'You look like you're floating on a daybed in a pool.'

'Except for this, of course.' She gave his butt a little kick with her feet. 'This posture would not be suitable poolside.'

'True.' He withdrew slowly and drove into her with renewed purpose to prove it. Over and over. Hard thrusts. Long thrusts. Making her body wind tight with every exquisite movement.

His thumb circled her clit, light flicks alternating

with deeper pressure, keeping time as he pumped into her. She watched him touching her, watched him driving into her, more turned on than she'd ever been.

The pleasure built as he picked up speed, pounding into her so hard that her elbows knocked the headboard repeatedly.

'Hudson…' Her body stiffened, spasmed, as she came on a low moan, echoed by him a second later.

Boneless, she unlocked her legs, and he collapsed on top of her, generous to a fault even now as he rolled his weight to one side so as not to crush her.

'Have I made you late for work?' he mumbled against her neck, nipping the tender skin below her ear.

'All good,' she said, too sated to move but knowing that Remy would kill her if she rocked up late for the second morning in a row. 'In fact, I have time for a shower, if you'd like to join me?'

'You'll be late.' He nuzzled her, making her skin pebble as his hand drifted up her thigh, his fingertips skating across her stomach, before coming to rest a fraction away from her mound. 'Better ring ahead and let them know now.'

Makayla did exactly that.

CHAPTER FOURTEEN

THE END OF the week couldn't come quick enough for Hudson.

Usually, he dreaded weekends for the simple fact he worked long hours at the theatre followed by busy nights at the club.

This weekend would be different.

He had a date lined up with Mak, a step back in time, that he hoped would solidify what he already knew.

They were frigging great together.

Being a couple hadn't interfered with their work. If anything, her dancing had moved to a new level, filled with a passion and grace found lacking in many on stage these days. Or maybe he was just biased and saw sensuousness in her every move considering they'd spent every night this week wrapped in each other's arms.

He couldn't get enough and, thankfully, the feeling was entirely mutual.

'Hey, Hudson, how's it hanging?' The booming voice of Reg Grober, Sydney's leading backer of every single show to hit Australian shores, rang out across the stage as the tall, grey-haired power broker strode towards him. 'Unearthed any stars lately?'

Hudson had gained something of a reputation over the last few years for taking unknown talent and casting them in well-known stage musicals, only to find their star taking off. He prided himself on his eye for talent and was proud to call Reg a friend.

He might have a great job managing Embue and knew he could always count on his bestie Tanner, but he'd learned from a young age that jobs weren't always rock solid and people weren't always dependable. He viewed Reg as a security blanket, a contact that could come in handy one day if the bottom of his world ever fell out, as it had before.

'I've got a new show starting next week at the nightclub I manage. Some great performers there. You should come see.' He shook Reg's hand when he stuck it out. 'Let me know which night and I'll leave your name on the door.'

'I might just do that.' Reg gestured around the empty theatre. 'Can't believe we've had a sell-out here for the duration. Who knew people liked musicals about Aussie icons at the beach?'

'Whatever you touch turns to gold, mate.'

Reg acknowledged the compliment with a broad grin. 'Speaking of gold, know any outstanding dancers? I'm involved in a start-up on Broadway and one of the chorus busted her leg. We need someone good to start over there in a month.'

Hudson's heart pounded in his chest, making him

oddly breathless. He knew a dancer, one of the best, whose dream was to star on Broadway.

However, when he'd told her he might have contacts to help her get there he'd never anticipated it would be so soon.

If he put Mak's name forward, she could leave him in a month.

Four short weeks.

And they'd be over before they'd really begun.

For a long moment, he considered lying. But this was *Mak* and he couldn't do it to her, no matter how selfish he was and wanted to keep her to himself for a little longer.

'I do know someone. She'd be perfect.'

Reg beamed. 'Great. We'll be auditioning in a week so I'll send you the details.' He tapped the side of his nose. 'And I'll make sure to be completely unbiased, even though I know that anyone you send me will have an automatic walk-up role.'

'Thanks, Reg.' Hudson shook his hand again and waved the clipboard in his free one. 'Got to get back to work.'

'Sure thing, I'll leave you to it.'

As Reg walked away, Hudson knew he should call Mak and share the good news. He delved into his pocket, pulled out his cell and brought up her name. However, his thumb hovered on the call button as a host of unwelcome thoughts flooded him.

Once she found out, would she end this thing between them now to focus on her big break?

Would she stay with him for the next few weeks out of obligation, as a thank-you for getting her the job?

Or the biggie, if he laid it all on the line, would she still leave him regardless?

Hudson hated secrets. He'd grown up with them. Keeping his father's alcoholism from the schoolteachers and welfare workers. Watching men cheat on their wives in the strip clubs. Seeing women whoring. A world of secrets that festered and left him feeling tainted because of it.

He couldn't keep this secret from Mak to suit his own ends.

He glared at her name on the screen, clutching the cell so tight he wouldn't have been surprised if it cracked.

He would tell her.

He had to tell her.

Later.

Hating himself, he slipped the phone back in his pocket and focussed on ensuring this production went off without a hitch, unable to shake the feeling that in making all Mak's dreams come true he was ruining his.

CHAPTER FIFTEEN

'I THINK I liked you better before you were getting laid regularly,' Charlotte said, perched on her favourite stool in the window at Le Miel. 'You're way too smug.'

Makayla grinned at her flatmate and placed a steaming hot chocolate in front of her. 'Can't blame a girl for being satisfied.'

Charlotte held up her hand. 'Please. Spare me the details.'

'Lucky for you, I'm not one to shag and tell.' Makayla winked. 'Anything else I can get you?'

'One of those decadent *beignets*.' Charlotte pointed at the display cabinet where Abby's amazing creations made every customer's mouth water. 'And throw in a *pain au chocolat* too.'

Makayla's eyebrows rose. 'Hungry?'

'Drowning my sorrows in pastry.' Charlotte sighed and slumped a little. 'That new boss I mentioned? The one working remotely so I can't even tell him what I really think of him to his face? He's making my life hell.'

'So quit. You're diligent and there must be stacks of jobs for good accountants.'

A flicker of fear flashed across Charlotte's face. 'Nerdy introverts don't do well making grand gestures like quitting before we have a new job to go to.'

'Then start hunting. Or better yet, sign up with one of those agencies that'll find you a dream job just like that.' She snapped her fingers. Yeah, like it was that easy. She'd registered with every talent agency on the eastern seaboard for years and she knew first-hand that dream jobs were few and far between. But Charlotte looked so morose she had to pump her up somehow. 'No boss should make you this unhappy.'

Charlotte's eyes narrowed but not before Makayla glimpsed a wicked gleam. 'Unlike your boss, who's making you exceedingly happy.'

'Hudson's a great guy,' she said, her dismissive shrug belying just how great he was.

Work-wise, he knew his stuff and he treated her with nothing but professionalism. He demanded perfection from his crew and ran to a rigid schedule. She liked working with a boss who respected his dancers and knew what he was doing.

But away from rehearsals, Hudson was simply… amazing.

He made her feel cherished in a way she'd never had with a guy. His main goal seemed to be giving her pleasure, and she returned the favour and then some.

But she'd learned the hard way that if something was too good to be true it usually was and she knew this fledgling relationship wouldn't end well.

And it would end. There was no doubt. She'd never lost sight of her goal, making it on Broadway, all these years. Every audition she attended, every dress rehearsal, every dance show no matter how small the crowd, had been part of her grand plan.

She could never give it all up for a guy, no matter how special. Especially one who had let her down badly once before.

They might have lain the past to rest but a small part of her deep down still resented him for not giving her an explanation for his behaviour that night.

She'd deliberately pushed the memory of his unwarranted freak-out to the back of her mind since they'd got together, not wanting to spoil the amazing fun—both in and out of the bedroom—they were having.

But having that residual doubt, no matter how deep she'd buried it, still niggled. Would she be foolishly setting herself up for a fall if she threw herself wholeheartedly into a relationship with Hudson?

Her heart encouraged trust, her head screamed logic that couldn't be denied.

He'd left her once without an explanation.

He could do it again.

'You're so lucky to have found a guy like Hudson.' Charlotte rested her chin in her hand, whimsical as usual, her eyes dreamy as she envisioned a hero out of one of those novels she couldn't put down.

'Someone talking about my right-hand man?'

Makayla stiffened as Tanner appeared behind her and draped an arm across her shoulders. 'Hud is a great guy and I've never seen him so happy, so I'm guessing that has something to do with you? He won't give me any details, which is a pain in the ass because I want to hang shit on him but can't. Maybe you'll give me the low-down?'

Heat suffused her cheeks as she shrugged off his arm and elbowed him in the ribs. 'I'm not saying a word.' She made a zipping motion over her lips. 'And leave him alone.'

'Protective too, I respect that.' Tanner winked at Charlotte, who always appeared shell-shocked that a guy as hot as Tanner was talking to her. 'Ain't love grand?'

'You should know, bozo, considering you're gaga over Abby,' Makayla said, chalking a point up in the air.

She didn't need to see Tanner's goofy grin to know the guy was head over heels for her best friend.

'Hey, here's an idea.' Tanner's gaze turned positively evil. 'We should double date some time. You and Hud, me and Abby. That way, I'll get the low-down first-hand.'

'Not going to happen.' Makayla hesitated, not wanting to make a big deal over the fact her relationship with Hudson was a secret, but having to tell her friends so they wouldn't accidentally hassle her in front of the wrong people, like the show's cast. 'Hudson and I are keeping this thing between us secret.'

Tanner and Charlotte wore matching comical WTF expressions so she continued. 'He cast me as the lead in his show so I don't want rumours starting that I slept with the boss to score the role.'

Understanding sparked in Tanner's eyes. 'Good point. I won't say a word.'

'And I've got no one to tell,' Charlotte added, sounding morose.

'I'll leave you ladies to it.' Tanner backed away, hands up, as if he didn't want to be on the receiving end of a lecture. 'But for what it's worth, I approve of you and Hud getting together. I've never seen him like this, relaxed and approachable. You're good for him.'

Before she could respond, Tanner swivelled and strode away, leaving Makayla more worried than ever.

They hadn't actually spelled out the boundaries of their relationship, beyond keeping it secret. Did Hudson understand they had an expiration date? That she would ultimately head overseas to pursue her dream?

'What's wrong?' Charlotte touched her arm, concern creasing her brow. 'You look like you've choked on a croissant.'

'This love stuff is tough,' Makayla said, propping on a stool, wishing her shift could end now so she could head home and hide away in the apartment to mull this latest development.

Charlotte's eyebrows shot heavenward. 'You love him?'

Startled, she shook her head. 'No. Just a figure of speech.'

She couldn't afford to fall in love with anyone right now, least of all Hudson. He'd broken her heart once by walking away from her, had seriously hurt her. She didn't want to return the favour but that was exactly what she would do when she ended this.

If love entered the equation for either of them, it would be disastrous.

'Have you ever had a serious relationship?'

Charlotte snorted and gestured at her sedate outfit of grey trousers, white blouse and flat pumps. 'Do I look like the type of woman to inspire grand passions in any man?'

'Don't sell yourself short,' she said. 'Any guy would be lucky to have you.'

'Yeah, tell that to the hundreds of hotties batting down my door.'

Makayla grinned at her friend's dry response. 'So that's a no, then? No serious relationships?'

'No relationships, period.' Charlotte sighed and shifted on her stool, uncomfortable. 'I dated occasionally in uni. Fellow accountancy students. No muss, no fuss kind of guys that were boring as hell.' She shook her head. 'At the risk of sounding like a cliché from one of those fabulous romances I read, I need a bad boy. Some big, bold, annoying, arrogant guy to rattle my cage.'

Makayla bit back her first retort, that the kind of guy Charlotte described would break her heart faster than she could say number-cruncher. 'Trust me, sweetie, you'll meet some great guy when you least expect it.'

Charlotte rolled her eyes. 'Yeah, and I'll morph into a sexy siren too.'

Makayla chose her next words carefully, not wanting to offend. 'We could do a makeover if you like? Play around with some different looks? Change it up a little with hair and make-up?'

Charlotte wrinkled her nose as if the milk in her

hot chocolate had curdled. 'All that stuff just isn't me. Besides, when I meet a guy I want him to like me for me, not because of a few fake eyelashes and hair extensions.'

Makayla could relate. Hudson knew about her past, knew her faults, but liked her regardless. He'd even moved past his freak out of seeing her strip and that kind of acceptance was rare.

Hudson was a keeper. Pity she wouldn't be the one doing the keeping.

Makayla glanced at her watch and pulled a face. 'I have to get back to work.'

'Sure.' Charlotte pointed at the cabinet. 'Starting with serving me those pastries I ordered.'

Makayla smiled. 'Whichever guy is lucky enough to have you, I hope he has a French pastry addiction like you do.'

'If he doesn't, I'll convert him.' Charlotte hid a smile behind the mug as she lifted the hot chocolate to her lips, but Makayla recognised bittersweet when she saw it.

Charlotte was a homebody. The kind of woman who coveted the girly dream of a husband, kids, dog and a mortgage. From the way she kept their apartment spotless and whipped up comfort meals, she'd make a good wife. Makayla hoped that in chasing her dream, she didn't get her heart trampled on by some jerk in the process.

'One *beignet* and *pain au chocolat* coming up.'

However, as Makayla served Charlotte her order,

then headed back to the kitchen, her thoughts circled back to what Tanner had said earlier.

She made Hudson happy, and Tanner had never seen him like that.

How happy would Hudson be when she walked away?

CHAPTER SIXTEEN

'WHEN YOU SAID we'd be eating the best burgers in town, I had no idea you'd bring me here.' Makayla stared around the run-down diner in the heart of Kings Cross, her eyes alight with joy. 'It's been at least six years since I last had one of Jonnie's specials.'

'That's what I thought,' he said, leaning against the faded red vinyl seat in a booth in the far corner near the jukebox. 'You rarely ate burgers back then anyway, always watching your weight.'

She crinkled her nose in disgust. 'Yeah, it almost became an obsession, until Mum talked sense into me.'

'Dancers need to be fit, not stick insects.' He snagged her hand across the table and lifted it to his lips. 'Besides, I happen to think you've got a sensational bod and I wouldn't change a thing.'

'Sweet talker,' she muttered, grinning when he brushed a kiss across the back of her hand before releasing it. 'I'm way too curvy for a dancer but I bust my ass working out in the gym and jogging daily to ensure I can still score the roles I want.'

Guilt lodged in his chest, as heavy as a stone, and he resisted the urge to rub it away.

He still hadn't mentioned the Broadway role Reg had told him about. The audition was a few days away and he knew he had to tell her. But he'd been looking forward to this date, to a stroll down memory lane, too much to spoil it.

Because he knew what would happen the moment he told Mak about the audition. She'd become obsessed, wanting to research the show, rehearse and focus on the biggest break of her career.

He didn't blame her. He would do the same. But that small stubborn part of him deep inside resisted telling her, at least for another day.

He would lose her. Nothing surer. He'd spent a lifetime doing right by other people; he could be a selfish prick for a few more hours.

'Is everything okay?'

He stiffened. He should be glad she could read him so well but it didn't help the guilt eating away at him. 'Yeah, why?'

'You keep drifting off the last two days, like you've got something on your mind?'

'Only you.' This time, when he reached for her hand, he didn't let go. 'I've never had a real relationship before and it's kinda distracting.'

'I know the feeling,' she said, giving his hand a squeeze. 'I need to focus on opening night next week and making sure my footwork in the final samba is perfect, but sometimes at rehearsal I find myself thinking of other things.'

A cute blush stained her cheeks, making him want to haul her across the table and do wicked things to her.

'Like?'

The blush deepened. 'Like the way you take me in the shower every morning. Like the way you're so eager we barely make it to your bedroom most nights.'

The tip of her tongue darted out to moisten her bottom lip, an innocuous action that shot straight to his already hard cock. 'Like the way you use your tongue to make me forget every goddamn thing.'

Hudson shifted in the booth, trying to ease the constriction in his jeans. Yeah, like moving around would do that. Buried deep in Mak or being sucked dry by her luscious mouth was the only way to ease his aching cock.

'Do you have any idea what you do to me?' He threaded his fingers between hers. 'I'm tempted to say screw the burgers and let's get out of here.'

'You're hard?' She quirked an eyebrow, feigning innocence, and he bit back a groan. 'Pity these old booths don't have tablecloths.' A wicked smile curved her lips. 'I could've taken care of that little problem for you.'

'There's nothing little about my problem and you know it.'

'Modest, much?'

They laughed and this time it wasn't guilt making his chest heavy but his heart, doing some weird flip-flop that made breathing difficult.

This was what he'd always imagined it would be like between them. Friends who became lovers and it only solidified their bond. The kind of connection born of years of shared confidences. The kind of relationship bred from trust.

But she hadn't always trusted him. Not enough to tell him the entire truth, like that night indelibly etched on his brain when she'd ripped the blinkers from his eyes.

Now he was doing the same, withholding information from her.

What did that say about their relationship?

'Why did you start stripping?'

Damn, the question popped out before he could censor it, or at least dress it up in better terms.

Predictably, she tugged her hand free of his, wariness descending over her expression as it blanked.

'Is that why you brought me here, to bring up the past?' Her upper lip curled in disgust. 'You thought plying me with burgers like old times would get me to spill my guts?'

Shit. He'd blurted the question at a vulnerable moment, desperate to discover something that had bugged him for years. But in doing so he'd driven a wedge between them. So much for a day of sweet reminiscing.

'Our date here has nothing to do with me trying to soften you up,' he said, showing his palms to her like he had nothing to hide. 'I guess the closer we get, the more I don't want anything tainting what we have. And while we've moved past that night, I hate that it happened in the first place. That it's this thing between us, like an elephant in the room that we keep ignoring.'

Her eyes blazed with anger as she leaned forward, resting her forearms on the table. 'Do you have any idea what you did to me, saying all that hurtful stuff that night you saw me stripping before walking out of my life?'

She shook her head, but not before he glimpsed the sheen of tears.

Fuck. He'd made her cry.

'That night I saw you at Le Chat, I freaked because I didn't want that kind of life for you—'

'It wasn't your call to make,' she said, her voice barely above a hiss. 'You didn't question my motivation. You didn't ask for an explanation. Instead, you jumped to conclusions and judged me for it.'

She dragged a hand through her hair, making his palms itch to do the same. 'God, Hudson, I missed you so much. You were my best friend back then, the only person who really got me and suddenly you weren't there any more.'

She tapped at her chest. 'It was like you stuck a knife right here and I never recovered.'

Hudson never cried but for the first time in a long time, he felt the burn of tears. 'I'm so, so sorry. A lot of what I said that night had nothing to do with you and more to do with my own shit.'

She lifted her head a fraction, studying him with curiosity. 'What do you mean?'

Hudson had never told anyone about his mother. About his early suspicions, later solidified into the horrible truth. As a young kid he'd watched her spiral downhill, from a respectable waitress, to a stripper, to something far worse he'd discovered later…

It had killed him inside, watching the woman he idolised walk away from him without looking back.

That was the real reason he'd fought with Mak that fateful night, unable to stick around to watch her follow the same downtrodden path.

Losing his mum had devastated him. Losing Mak the same way would've finished him off.

So he'd removed himself completely, had cut ties with her and hadn't looked back.

He could trust her with the truth but something held him back. Some long-seated, deeply buried, self-protective mechanism that screamed he couldn't trust anyone, least of all the woman he'd hurt and who had the potential to hurt him right back.

'I'd been working the clubs, doing odd jobs, since I was ten. You knew that.' He rubbed a hand over his face. It did little to ease the tension. 'I saw too many women fall into the temptation of easy money by stripping. Then it became harder and they couldn't walk away. Some turned to drugs, others took the next step…' He trailed off, horrified when her expression turned glacial, as if she'd never look at him the same way again.

'I hated seeing you up there. Hated that you hadn't turned to me if you needed money. Hated that you hadn't trusted me enough to confide in me before you did it—'

'You're a moron,' she said, her tone low and lethal. 'Do you think I wanted to take my clothes off for a roomful of slobbering sleaze-bags? I needed the money fast to pay for Mum's funeral. She deserved that at least, after all the sacrifices she made for me over the years. So I accepted that job for one night. That's it.'

Sick to his stomach, he stared at the woman he'd misjudged, searching for the right thing to say and coming up empty.

'I saw how hard you worked, how desperate you were to escape the Cross, so no way in hell I would've approached you for that kind of money.' She shook her head, her glorious red hair tumbling over her shoulders and semi-shielding her face. 'I was ashamed of how far I had to go to get that money and no way in hell would I have told you about it. Then you walked in that night and you were a prick to me.'

'Fuck, I really messed up.' He rested his hands on the table, palms down, needing some kind of anchor in a world suddenly tipped on its ass. 'I wish I could turn back time and do it differently that night but I can't. I'm an idiot. But know that I was trying to protect you from a life you didn't deserve.'

The fury twisting her mouth eased. 'You're right about one thing. You're an idiot.'

'Was.' He tried a tentative smile. 'I'd like to think I'm smarter these days.'

'Debatable.' When she placed her hands over his, the tight band of anxiety squeezing his chest dissolved. 'So now that we've confronted the elephant, can we shoo him away and concentrate on the here and now?'

Hudson would like nothing better, but guilt still gnawed at him. He'd misjudged her badly that fateful night, had let his own preconceptions colour his judgement and make him jump to conclusions.

He felt like an idiot. Pissed too, that she hadn't come to him because he'd made such a big deal out of escaping the Cross. He'd known how she felt about stripping, how she'd vowed to make it as a dancer without having to do it, yet he hadn't trusted her enough and had jumped to conclusions.

He should've known there had to be something big behind her decision to strip that night; he should've given her the benefit of the doubt.

Unfortunately he couldn't change the past, but he could make up for it by giving her the future she'd always dreamed of.

'Speaking of here and now, I've got some news you may like.'

She quirked an eyebrow, and he continued. 'Don't get your hopes up because nothing may come of this, but remember I mentioned I have contacts in the theatre industry?'

Her fingers involuntarily dug into his hands as she leaned forward a fraction. 'Yeah?'

'You've heard of Reg Grober?'

Her eyes widened. 'He's huge. Backs all the major theatre productions here and many overseas.'

'I ran into him yesterday and he mentioned an opening for a dancer in his latest show on Broadway. Asked me if I knew anyone—'

'Oh, my God, you didn't?'

'I did.' He grinned as she released his hands to clap hers in excitement. 'The audition is next week but Reg trusts my judgement, so you should be in with a good chance. In fact, I think he said that anyone I recommend would be a walk-in.'

She flopped back against the booth seat, her expression incredulous, two spots of colour staining her cheeks.

'You're serious?'

'Would I kid about something as important as this?' He smiled as he glimpsed the shimmer of tears in her eyes. 'I know this is your dream.'

'I—I don't know what to say…' She stood and moved around to his side of the booth, shooing him over.

When he moved over, she slid in next to him and flung her arms around him, burrowing into the crook of his neck. 'Thank you.'

'You're welcome.' He slid his arms around her and held her close, inhaling the tempting vanilla fragrance of her hair, wishing they could stay this way forever.

But all too soon she pulled away, returned to her seat and their burgers arrived. They ate, traded banter and swapped trade talk as they usually did.

Yet beneath it all Hudson could feel an undercurrent, a powerful force pulling Mak away from him.

He knew he'd done the right thing in telling her about the Broadway audition, even if it had been out of guilt.

But at what cost?

CHAPTER SEVENTEEN

MAKAYLA KNEW SHE should be listening to Hudson as they strolled the familiar back streets of Kings Cross, but her mind kept drifting back to the news he'd given her, casual as you like, over dinner.

He'd put her forward for an audition with Reg Grober. *The* Reg Grober. For a dance role on Broadway.

Freaking *Broadway*!

She'd pinched herself several times when he hadn't been looking then proceeded to digest one of Jonnie's famous burgers without tasting a thing. She could've been ingesting arsenic sprinkled on a mud pie for all the attention she'd paid her food.

Broadway.

Her dream from the first moment she'd slipped on tap shoes at age three.

Her mum had never laughed at her. Instead, she'd fostered her love of dance, scrimping and saving from her own jobs, as a part-time waitress and dancer, to pay for lessons. Jazz, tap, ballet, Makayla had done them all. And she'd practised until her toes bled, repeating routines in front of the cracked second-hand mirror in their tiny lounge room in a one-bedroom flat on top of Bluey's bar in Darlinghurst Road.

Though they'd lived in the heart of Kings Cross and Makayla had grown up around dive bars, her mum had instilled values in her from a young age. She might have seen stuff a kid shouldn't but she could never do those things herself.

That was part of why Hudson's misjudgement of her that one and only night she'd stripped had stung so damn bad. Makayla wouldn't have done it unless she was desperate, and he should've known that.

But after their earlier discussion it looked as if they'd finally moved past that night. He'd freaked out because he was trying to protect her. Good intentions, bad execution.

They'd cleared the air before he'd dropped his little bombshell.

And she hadn't been able to focus on anything else since.

'Hey, are you listening to me?'

She laughed and squeezed his hand. 'Honestly? I have no idea how far we've walked and I haven't heard half of what you've said.' She did a little jig on the spot. 'I can't stop thinking about the audition.'

'I knew you'd be like this when I told you.' He grinned and swung their arms between them as they resumed walking. 'You're nothing if not predictable.'

'Hey, I resent that,' she said, bumping him with her hip.

However, he missed the wall and stumbled into a

small opening between two buildings, tugging her with him. It could've passed for an alley if it weren't so narrow, barely enough room for the two of them. A snug fit. Snugger when she pressed against him and his back hit the wall.

'Predictable, huh?' She ground against him a little, his cock rubbing her sweet spot and making her breath hitch. 'Want me to show you how non-predictable I can be?'

Makayla had done many things in her lifetime. Sex in public wasn't one of them. But they were in a back alley, secluded from prying eyes. No one ever strolled this way. In fact, the only reason why they'd taken this route was because they'd done it years earlier, when he'd walked her home many times, defiantly confident that nobody would lay a finger on them because he was so well known in the Cross.

'You're serious?' His eyes glittered with excitement in the wan light spilling through the alley opening.

'Well, I need to dispel this preconception you have of me,' she said, snaking her hand between their bodies to cup his burgeoning boner. 'And what better way than to ravish you in an alley?'

She rubbed the length of him, savoured his low groan. 'Hot, fast, alley sex. What could be less predictable than that?'

He claimed her mouth in response, their teeth clashing a little in his eagerness to devour her. His tongue swept into her mouth, commanding and demanding, teasing and taunting until she strained against him, needing more.

She'd never been so thankful for wearing a dress when he rucked up the skirt, a firm hand kneading her ass while the other delved beneath her panties to finger her hot spot.

'I love how responsive you are,' he murmured against her ear, nipping the soft skin beneath it as he slid one finger inside her, another, while his thumb worked magic on her clit. 'So tight. So wet…'

She moaned as his thumb increased pressure, driving her to the brink faster than she could've thought possible. She had no idea if it was the fear of being seen, the bite of chill against her naked butt, or her being so confident in Hudson's ability to pleasure her, but whatever it was, her orgasm built quickly, making her quiver and strain towards it.

She clung to him as his thumb changed the angle on her clit slightly and pushed harder, faster, and she was gone. She sank her teeth into his shoulder as she came, pleasure spiralling upward and outward, wave upon wave until she sagged limp against him.

She was barely aware of him rummaging in his pocket, unzipping and sheathing. But she knew what was coming and her body tensed in anticipation.

When he pressed against her, she hooked a leg around his waist, giving him all the access he needed to drive into her in one hard thrust.

Maybe it was the narrowness of the alley and the angle of their bodies, maybe it was the wantonness of the situation, maybe it was the heightened awareness of outdoor sex, but she'd never felt so turned on in all her life.

With every thrust she came alight, ripples of awareness spreading through her and making her tingle, her skin hypersensitive to his every touch, her body finely attuned to his in a way it had never been.

Every inch of her craved, every nerve ending buzzed. She'd turned into one of those static electricity balls, sparking wherever he touched her.

'You wanted hard and fast, right?'

'Yeah…' she gasped as he drove into her harder, faster, the beginnings of another orgasm teasing at the edges of her consciousness.

'What the lady wants,' he murmured, grabbing her ass and picking her up, angling her just right so she came apart again, so swiftly and spontaneously that she let out a yell he quickly silenced by covering her mouth with his.

He stiffened a moment later, and she swallowed his groan, the power of his orgasm making her wish they could do this all over again.

But all too quickly he'd lowered her until her feet touched the ground. Withdrew. Smoothed down her skirt before turning away to take care of business. While all Makayla could do was prop against the wall until the wobble in her legs subsided.

When he turned back, his grin lit up the alley. 'That was…' he shook his head, momentarily lost for words '…the hottest damn thing ever.'

He reached for her, hugged her tight. 'You're incredible, you know that?'

'Tell me something I don't know.'

Her sassy retort earned a chuckle, his chest reverberating against hers, before he eased back.

'Have you worked up an appetite for dessert? Perhaps we can have a nightcap and apple pie at Bluey's?'

'I'd like that,' she said, searching his face for some sign that what had just happened between them meant as much to him as it did to her.

She'd just had the hottest sex of her life—in public—which made her realise something: she never would've trusted any other guy this much.

Hudson made her feel cherished and safe and, dare she say it, loved.

It frightened the hell out of her.

She couldn't lose sight of her goal, especially when it could be within her grasp. If all went according to plan and she nailed the audition for Reg Grober she could be moving to New York sooner rather than later, and falling for Hudson would only complicate matters.

She couldn't fall in love with him.

She wouldn't.

But what if it was too late?

CHAPTER EIGHTEEN

HUDSON HADN'T BEEN a monk over the years. Being a manager in Sydney's hippest club ensured he never had any shortage of beautiful women wanting a piece of him. It didn't make him conceited. It was a fact he accepted with eternal gratitude.

But never in the years since he'd lost his virginity at fifteen to a much older woman who ran a bar in the Cross had he indulged in the kind of risqué sex he'd just had with Mak.

She'd blown his mind. Literally.

He'd brought her to the Cross for a stroll down memory lane. Never in his wildest dreams had he anticipated raunchy alley sex.

He'd never felt like this. Totally discombobulated. Mak constantly surprised him, with a knack for throwing him off-guard regularly. It made him wonder; did she do it on purpose, to keep him at an emotional distance? His musing was soon replaced by a darker supposition.

Had the phenomenal sex been her way of repaying him for the Grober audition?

He hated the mere thought of it, as it cheapened what they'd shared ten minutes ago. He didn't want her to feel grateful. Or as if she owed him anything.

What would she think if she knew he'd only blurted the news about the audition out of guilt for being such a prick in the past?

She'd reacted the way he'd anticipated too, her mind drifting and her responses vague, already pulling away from him. If they hadn't stumbled into that alley, would she have wanted to spend the rest of the evening with him or would she already be home, researching the Broadway show and all it entailed?

He hated feeling like this. Confused and concerned. So he'd done the only thing he could think of to re-establish equilibrium; brought her to Bluey's and hoped that memories of their shared past would strengthen the bonds between them now.

'How long since you've been here?' He held the door open for her and waited until she entered before following.

'Too long,' she said, rapidly blinking as she glanced around the bar. 'I can't believe it looks the same.'

'You know Bluey. If it ain't broke, don't fix it.' He guided her through the throng of late-night jazz fans that crowded the bar.

Every table was full and the standing-room area near the stage had people ten deep. Hudson was glad. A packed house would keep Bluey busy and hopefully not focussed on his impending trip to see the big guy upstairs.

'It even smells the same,' Mak said, inhaling deeply and closing her eyes. 'Fried onion rings and bourbon.'

Hudson knew what she meant. Every place he'd ever worked back then had its own smell, some more pleasant than others. Bluey's had always smelled good to him because he knew he'd find Mak here, holed up in a small room off the main bar. Doing homework. Flicking through magazines. Keeping busy while her mum worked a shift.

He touched her hand when he spotted Bluey. 'I spy someone who would love to see you.'

Her eyes opened and zeroed in on the hallway leading from the main bar to the back. 'Oh, my God, he looks awful.'

'You might need to keep that gem to yourself,' he said, guiding her towards Bluey, whose eyes lit up the moment he spied them. 'Bloody cancer. So unfair.'

'He looks skeletal,' she murmured, reaching for Hudson's hand and holding on tight. 'Poor Bluey.'

However, as they neared him, she pasted a smile on her face, released Hudson's hand and enveloped the older man in a hug. 'It's been too long.'

'You got that right, girlie.' Bluey's arms wrapped around her, and Hudson had to look away for fear the emotion clogging his throat would be too easily read on his face.

When they eventually disengaged, Hudson glanced back to find Bluey staring at Mak with tears in his eyes.

'You're the spitting image of your mother.' He reached out to touch her hair. 'Even the same striking colour.'

'Mum was beautiful so I guess I'm lucky.'

'She sure was.' Bluey cleared his throat and gestured at the bar. 'What'll you have to drink?'

'Chardonnay for me, please.' She glanced at Hudson. 'You?'

Hudson needed something stronger tonight, something that would chase away his funk and the insistent rumblings deep inside that he'd already lost Mak.

'Whisky, neat.'

Bluey's eyebrows raised in comical disbelief. 'First time you've ever had a man's drink in all these years.'

'I'm shaking things up tonight.' Hudson shot Mak a meaningful look, and she blushed.

Bluey snorted and poked Mak in the arm. 'Word of advice, girlie. Don't let this fool sweet talk you.'

'Might be too late for that,' she said, smiling as she slid an arm around his waist and rested her head against his shoulder. 'He's kinda charming when he wants to be.'

Bluey snorted again, unable to hide a grin. 'I'll be right back with those drinks. Make yourself comfortable in the nook.'

'So you think I'm charming, huh?' He backed her into the nook where they'd once spent countless hours chatting and nuzzled her neck. 'Because you ain't seen nothing yet.'

'Hmm…' She almost purred as he nibbled his way across her jaw, down her neck, to the tender spot above her shoulder. 'Want to hear something perverted?'

He lifted his head to stare at her. 'Always.'

'What you're doing now, here? I used to fantasise about it happening a lot back then.' An adorable blush stained her cheeks. 'And I filled an awful lot of notebooks with our initials intertwined in hearts when everyone thought I was doing homework.'

Nostalgia gripped him, squeezing his chest in a vice. 'Your crush was reciprocated one hundred per cent but the age thing...'

'Yeah, I know. Everybody would've flipped if we'd started dating back then.' A cheeky glint darkened her eyes. 'Especially if we were as naughty then as we are now.'

'Naughty doesn't begin to describe it,' he said, his cock instantly at half-mast at the mention of what they'd indulged in less than twenty minutes earlier.

'Then maybe we can think up other words. Later.' She arched her pelvis into his, her smile positively wicked.

'You're insatiable,' he muttered, brushing a kiss across her lips. 'And I like it. A lot.'

'For Pete's sake, get a room,' Bluey said, entering the nook and placing a tray with drinks on the table in the corner. 'I always pegged you for a smart girl, Mak. Don't know what you see in this bozo.'

'He has his good points.' She laughed and slipped out of his arms, before taking a seat at the table. 'One of them being the fact he doesn't forget his friends.'

She winced and reached to cover Bluey's hand with hers where it rested on the table. 'I'm sorry I haven't been around.'

'Shit happens.' Bluey shrugged but Hudson saw how much Mak's admission meant in the set of his jaw. 'You moved on after your mum died. A natural progression.'

'Yeah, but I should've popped in to visit.' The corners of her mouth downturned. 'Hudson told me. About the cancer.'

'Like I said, shit happens.' Bluey blinked a few times before his jaw clenched. 'I'm dying. So let's not waste this visit overstating the obvious and talk about other stuff.'

Bluey's gaze turned shifty. 'Tell me what's going on between you two.'

Mak said, 'Nothing,' at the same time as Hudson and Bluey laughed.

'Hey, I won't tell anyone.' Bluey tapped the side of his nose. 'What happens at Bluey's stays at Bluey's.'

Hudson waited for Mak to say something, not wanting to overstep and say the wrong thing: like the fact he was in a relationship with Mak but it could end at any moment.

Mak flashed a cheeky smile at them both. 'Hudson's sort of my boss at the moment so I'm not supposed to say anything, but…' She crooked her finger at Bluey. 'I had a massive crush on him years ago so you can't blame a girl for losing her head and falling for him a little.'

Hudson grinned. She'd admitted to falling for him. That had to be a good thing moving forward. So why did he feel like her admission was some kind of consolation prize considering she'd be leaving soon?

Bluey rolled his eyes. 'At least he's a good guy.'

'Thanks for that rousing endorsement.' Hudson

lifted his Scotch in a toast. 'To old times. And old timers.'

Bluey picked up his dark rum, his poison of choice for as long as Hudson could remember, and clinked glasses. 'To making the most of every minute.'

'To us,' Mak added, her simple toast meaning more than she could've imagined when she locked gazes with him, trying to convey a message he had no hope of interpreting.

Was she realising that his revelation earlier meant the end of them? That the odds were in her favour to pack up and head to New York without him? Did she care?

They'd never stipulated a time line for this relationship. Hell, they'd never spelled out much of anything. They'd given in to a long-held passion without articulating what this would mean if things got serious.

Because they'd both been stupid enough to believe it wouldn't.

After their first stupendous night together, Mak had said she wouldn't let a relationship stop her from achieving her career goals. He'd said he was happy to play this whatever way she wanted.

But what happened when Mak wanted to end this before it had really begun?

'Speaking of old times, want to hear something crazy?' Bluey slammed his glass down on the table a tad hard and winced. 'Because of the insane crush I had on your mum, I didn't touch your flat after she died and you moved out.'

'What?' Mak stilled, shock widening her eyes. 'You didn't rent it out to someone else?'

Bluey shook his head. 'Couldn't bear to change it.' He blushed and rubbed a hand over his face. 'At the risk of you thinking I'm a looney old man, I like going in there sometimes, reminiscing.'

'Wow.' Mak slumped back in her chair. 'Can I ask you something?'

'You can ask. I might not answer,' Bluey said, sounding embarrassed.

'Why didn't you ever tell Mum how you felt?'

'Are you kidding? She was way out of my league.' A deep frown slashed Bluey's brow. 'But there isn't a day that goes by now that I don't regret not having the balls to speak up and tell her.'

Something shifted in Hudson's chest, an uncomfortable flip-flop that left him wanting to rub away the odd ache. Did he have the balls to speak up? To tell Mak that, for him, this relationship was more than a transient thing?

He'd never been in a relationship that lasted beyond a few dates. Had never met a woman that captured his attention for longer than that. But Mak was the whole package. She entranced and captivated and totally bamboozled him on so many levels he wouldn't know where to start if he did try to articulate his feelings.

Initially, he'd thought the powerful pull between them had more to do with the past; that he'd finally got what he'd wanted and it was as good as he'd imagined.

But it was more than that and he knew it. Problem was, did she?

'For what it's worth, she never talked about guys but your name slipped into conversation often,' Mak said, patting Bluey's hand. 'In fact, I could've sworn you two might've had something going on in secret but were trying to shield me from it.'

Bluey's blush intensified and he swore under his breath. 'I wish. The closest I got to letting your mum know I was sweet on her was the requisite smooch on New Year's Eve.' A slow grin spread across his face. 'I always made sure she worked that shift.'

'Real smooth,' Hudson said, wishing Bluey had taken his chance when he'd had the opportunity.

Whatever happened with him and Mak, he'd never regret the time they'd spent together. But he still wanted more. He was greedy like that.

'You can go up and check out the flat if you like?' Bluey downed the rest of his rum. 'I need to get back out front.'

Mak's eyes lit up. 'I'd love to.'

Hudson hesitated, unsure whether to follow Bluey or stay with Mak. He didn't want to intrude on her stroll down memory lane but had the damnedest impulse to stay by her side. Like she was already slipping away if he let her out of his sight. Crazy.

Bluey waved as he headed into the main bar, leaving Hudson feeling like an extra wheel.

'Want to come with me?' Mak stood and held out her hand. 'Get a glimpse of my old bedroom, where I spent way too many hours lusting over you.'

He exhaled in relief and took her hand. 'You had exquisite taste.'

'Or way too much time on my hands and a woeful social life where I didn't get to meet any boys but you so—'

'Quit while you're ahead,' he said, tugging her into the corridor to sneak a kiss.

A long, deep, open-mouthed kiss that quickly escalated into his cock being hard and yearning to be inside her.

'We'll combust if we're not careful,' she whispered against the side of his mouth, kissing her way along his jaw towards his ear, where she nipped the lobe. 'I like how hot we are together.'

'Me too.' He ground against her to prove it, enjoying her soft mewl of pleasure. 'But doing it in the hallway of Bluey's seems almost sacrilegious.'

'Then let's get upstairs ASAP.' She tugged on his hand, half bounding up the stairs, leaving him no option but to follow, bemused and hopeful and incredibly horny.

He liked the fact she wanted him as much as he wanted her. That she'd instigated that frigging hot alley sex. But it seemed that whenever they entered emotional territory, like her admissions at the table a few minutes ago, she immediately reverted to the physical stuff. Whether as a distraction or a coping mechanism for feeling out of her depth, he had no idea.

He should question it. Ask her. But he couldn't formulate the words, with all his blood drained south. He'd ask. Later. Much later.

'I've never been up here,' he said when she paused outside a door at the top of the landing.

'Bluey never let anyone up here but his tenants.' She leaned against the door, her hand still gripping his. 'I almost plucked up the courage to invite you up here one day when Mum was out, but Bluey must've got an inkling of what I was up to because he invented some lame-ass job to send you on when you arrived and that was the end of that.'

'Better late than never, I guess.' They smiled at each other, goofy grins reflecting their shared pasts and how far they'd come.

'Come on, before this trip down memory lane makes me blubber.' She turned towards the door and tested the handle.

The door swung open and the first thing that hit him as they stepped inside was how clean the place was.

'Looks like Bluey has someone come in here once a week.'

'Yeah,' she said, so softly he barely heard.

When she tugged her hand free he released her, closing the door behind them as she drifted into the tiny apartment.

The place appeared threadbare: a frayed cotton two-seater sofa, cracked vinyl armchair, dining table for two, kitchenette. Two doors led from the sole room: one into a bathroom, the other into a bedroom.

Amazing that Mak and her mum hadn't got on each other's nerves in such a confined space. He'd had much more room at home but it hadn't helped his relationship with his father. It wouldn't have mattered if they'd had the entire continent between them—dear old dad would've found a way to make his life hell.

'It seems so much smaller now,' she said, as if reading his mind, slipping off her shoes to pad towards the bedroom. 'Mum always made me take my shoes off at the door. Said it was better for my dancer feet, to let them flex and extend naturally.'

'You've never felt the urge to come back here?'

It surprised him. For someone who loved her mum as much as Mak had, to go as far as stripping to get money for her funeral, that she hadn't been back to the place she grew up.

She shrugged and leaned in the bedroom doorway, her expression downcast. 'This place held no interest once Mum died. It wouldn't have mattered where we lived because Mum was home to me, not the apartment.'

'You're lucky you were so close.' He hesitated, before adding, 'I envy you that.'

'You've never thought of trying to find your mum?'

The familiar sick feeling deep in his gut that thoughts of his mum elicited made him wish he'd never come up here. He couldn't tell Mak the truth. Couldn't ruin this night, the evening she might have finally got her big break, and taint it with what he'd discovered when he'd gone in search of his mother. The truth had almost killed him. He didn't want Mak's pity. Not tonight. So after a lifetime of practice, he schooled his face into lack of interest. 'No point trying to find someone who doesn't want to be found.'

'Your dad never tried?'

'My dad's an asshole,' he snapped, instantly regretting his show of emotion for a subject that was off-limits.

He never discussed his shitty family life with anyone. Only Tanner had an idea of how bad things had been with his dad back then, but even his best friend didn't know the half of it.

Now, having Mak prod at a deep festering, well-hidden sore spot only served to reinforce what he already knew.

That his past had no right interfering with his future.

He worked his ass off so he could pay for his dad's special accommodation fees. He did his part. Even though the old bastard didn't deserve it.

He made the obligatory visits at Christmas and on his father's birthday—that was it, the extent of his familial obligations. Much easier to throw money at the problem and maintain his distance than be a sadist and inflict pain on himself that inevitably happened whenever he saw the old man.

Mak held up one hand and pretended to write on it with the other. 'Note to self. Avoid all talk of families.'

'Sorry.' He swiped a hand over his face. 'Sore point.'

'I gathered.' She crossed the tiny living room and held out her hands to him. 'Want the grand tour?'

He glanced around. 'Looks like I've seen most of it.'

'Not the bedroom.' She slipped her hands into his and stepped into his personal space, close enough that her nipples brushed his chest.

Just like that, he forgot his past and focussed on the here and now.

'Lead the way.' He backed her towards the bedroom, step by step, slow and steady, not breaking eye contact.

'What would you have done if I'd tried to lead you astray five years ago?' She batted her eyelashes, her smile coy.

'Being older and wiser, I would've been the ultimate gentleman, of course.' He paused in the doorway of the bedroom, quickly scanned the small interior. Two single beds. Uncomfortable but doable. Considering the alley hadn't posed any problems, a single bed wouldn't stop him.

'Lucky for me, you're not so wise any more.' She clutched at his shirt and tugged him close for a kiss. One of her signature 'I want to devour you as fast as humanly possible' kisses that never failed to leave him breathless and hard.

She had this way of using her tongue that drove him wild. Short thrusts, languid sweeps, keeping him guessing. Off-kilter and lusting.

'You sure this isn't too weird?' He backed her towards the nearest bed, hoping like hell she wouldn't renege now.

'Are you kidding? I fantasised about you being in here with me all the time back then.' She unzipped his fly and slid her hand inside, making him groan. 'I'd fall into bed at the end of a day, exhausted from homework and dance classes, too wired to sleep.'

She stroked the length of him, the gleam in her eyes

beyond wicked. 'So I'd imagine you here. Lying with me.' She rolled her thumb over the head of his cock and he tensed. 'Touching me.'

Carefully withdrawing her hand, she proceeded to unsnap the top button of his jeans and push them down his legs, along with his jocks. 'Lucky for me, the reality of you far surpasses my imagination back then.'

'Did you touch yourself while thinking of me?'

'Yeah. Just like this.' She blushed and slid her hands slowly down her front in response. Skimming her breasts. Tweaking her nipples. Before rucking up her dress and sliding her fingers under the elastic of her panties.

'Fuck me,' he said, mesmerised by the sight of Mak pleasuring herself.

'All in good time, my friend,' she said, her smile coy as she pushed her panties down, then returned to playing with herself.

Pushing her middle finger between her folds. Circling. Rubbing. Until her breathing altered, coming in short pants.

Torn between pleasure and pain, he gripped his cock, sliding his fist up and down, wanting to be inside her but unwilling to stop the erotic show.

'Would you like to finish me off?' She lifted her finger, glistening with moisture, towards him, like some prized offering, and his cock twitched.

He didn't have to be asked twice.

Thankful he'd had the foresight to start packing several condoms in his wallet since they'd started dating, he rolled one on in record time before hoisting her slightly and sliding in to the hilt. Savoured the first slide into tight, wet heat, slightly wondrous as she clenched around him, making him feel like a god-damn king.

It was like this every single time. So good. So bad, because he couldn't help but acknowledge the fleeting thought that each time could be their last and where the fuck would that leave him?

'I need to come now,' she said, her demand throaty, as she lifted one leg to rest her foot on the bed.

Determined to eradicate his doubts and focus on pleasure, he grabbed her ass, angled her forward so he dragged across her clit with every thrust.

'Oh, yeah, just like that.' Her head fell back as she arched her body against his in abandon, the sexiest damn thing he'd ever seen. Her skin sweat-slicked. Her lips parted. Her eyes glazed with passion. 'Now, Hudson. Now…'

He drove into her like a man possessed, oblivious to everything but the exquisiteness of being inside this woman. The mind-blowing ecstasy when his orgasm ripped through him like a freight train, shattering his barriers, exposing him like never before.

Mak yelled at the same time he did, her head snapping up so fast she almost knocked him out.

He didn't care. The only thing he cared about was keeping this woman in his life for longer than today, tomorrow and the day after that.

'I love—' Fuck, he'd almost slipped up and said he loved her. Too much too soon, if her startled expression was any indication. So he quickly added,

'—doing this,' throwing in a bashful half-shrug for good measure.

'Me too,' she said, brushing an all-too-brief peck on his lips before disengaging.

Uh-oh. Was her abrupt withdrawal a result of his botched admission or a figment of his imagination?

A knock on the door sounded, and her eyes widened in surprise. 'I'll get that.' She jerked her thumb over her shoulder. 'There's another door through to the bathroom if you need to tidy up.'

Considering he was standing there with a condom to be disposed of and naked from the waist down, that might be a good idea.

'Thanks,' he said, his heart sinking as she all but bolted from the bedroom.

Yeah, there was definitely something up. Just frigging great.

He heard murmured voices from the living room so slipped into the bathroom, closed the door to the lounge room and tidied up. When he heard the door close, he opened the bathroom door and peered into the living room. To find a veritable feast laid out on the small dining table.

She waved him over. 'I don't know whether to be appalled or grateful that Bluey sent this up, thinking we may have worked up an appetite.'

'He said that?'

She shook her head. 'No, he sent one of his minions up with the message and the food.'

'Crazy old coot.' As Hudson neared the table and

spied the food, his stomach rumbled. 'But remind me to thank him when we get downstairs.'

Bluey had sent up fried onion rings, buffalo wings, BBQ ribs and fries, with two gigantic pieces of apple pie and two bottles of lemonade.

'I'm starving,' Mak said, handing him a plate to dish up. 'Feels like I had that hamburger days ago.'

'I think we've worked off that meal twice,' he deadpanned, watching her reaction carefully, thankful when she laughed, the awkwardness of a few minutes ago gone.

'I've certainly worked up an appetite,' she said, piling her plate high before taking a seat at the table. 'Best workout ever.'

He held up his hand. 'I'm more than happy to assume the role of your personal trainer.' He winked. '*Very* personal trainer.'

'You're hired,' she said, raising a bottle of lemonade at him in a toast. 'To many sweaty workouts together.'

'I'll drink to that.' He clinked his lemonade bottle against hers and took a healthy swig. 'You really think Bluey sent us up here because he thought we'd fuck?'

'No idea, but considering the way you look at me it wouldn't take an Einstein to figure it out.' She picked up a wing and started gnawing on it with indelicate bites that made him laugh.

'And how do I look at you?'

'Like I'm this.' She brandished the wing. 'And you're particularly ravenous.'

He grinned and shrugged. 'A guy's gotta eat.'

'Yeah.' Her eyes darkened with passion, hopefully

remembering the many ways he'd eaten her since they'd got together.

'You need to stop looking at me like that,' he said, helping himself to some food. 'I need energy if you're about to pounce on me again.'

'Fair enough.' She made short work of the wing and consumed five ribs before he'd eaten a few onion rings.

'Wow, you really are hungry.'

'It's this food,' she said, gesturing at the diminishing feast. 'Bluey used to send up this stuff regularly for Mum and me if she'd pulled a double shift or danced at another club. He's so thoughtful.'

With that, a lone tear trickled down her cheek and she swiped it away with her free hand. 'Damn, being back here has me all sentimental.'

'I get it.'

And he did. He'd felt the same way when he'd come in to see Bluey last week yet he'd never lived here. How much worse must the nostalgia be for Mak?

'Being back here, in this flat, makes me realise perhaps I shouldn't have shunned my past so much.' She laid down a rib and wiped her hands on a napkin, her expression guarded. 'After Mum's funeral I got the hell out of the Cross and never looked back. But I shouldn't have done that.' She shook her head, her mouth downturned. 'I shouldn't have let that one night I stripped taint all the great memories of growing up here.'

'Is that why you left?'

She gnawed on her bottom lip, nodded. 'Yeah, I felt so dirty. I couldn't walk down the street any more without thinking every guy was leering at me, that they'd taken a front-row seat to my humiliation.' She held up her hand. 'And before you can apologise again, my leaving had nothing to do with your freak out.' She patted her chest. 'It was all me. But I shouldn't have ignored my past. I loved growing up in the Cross. This was my home and I felt safe. I should've kept in touch with Bluey. He was always so good to me.'

'He knows you care, in here.' He pointed to his heart. 'People who mean the most to us know how we feel about them even if we haven't seen them in ages and Bluey's one of the good guys. He knows how you feel.'

'Stop, you'll make me bawl,' she murmured, swiping a hand across her eyes. 'Did you know he used to buy my favourite teen magazines and leave them lying in the nook for when I got home from school?'

The image of big, bad Bluey raiding the local newsagent for teen magazines made Hudson smile. 'That's going above and beyond.'

'And not just that,' she said, her eyes glazed, lost in memories. 'He'd make sure the dance floor was clear for an hour a day after school so I could practise. No band rehearsals, no roadies doing sound checks, just me and my music.'

'He's a thoughtful guy.' Hudson didn't add that maybe Bluey had lavished affection on Mak because he'd never had kids of his own and he'd had a massive crush on her mum.

'He even lent me money once, when I wanted to buy Mum a special perfume for her birthday.' She pressed the pads of her fingertips to her eyes and took a few breaths, blowing out slowly. 'Doesn't seem fair, that I've only just reconnected and he'll be gone soon.'

Sadly, life wasn't fair. He knew that better than anyone. But Mak didn't need his cynicism right now.

'Bluey's a realist. And I think you are too. Life's hectic, for everyone. He gets it. Just pop in when you can. He'll appreciate it.'

He made it sound so simple when in reality if Mak nailed the Grober audition she'd be heading overseas sooner rather than later. But he didn't want to think about that now and he certainly didn't want that putting a dampener on what was left of this evening.

'Who made you so wise?' She balled her serviette and threw it at him.

He caught it and waggled a finger at her. 'I've always been wise, babe. Took you long enough to wake up to it.'

She poked her tongue out at him, grabbed a few fries and swiped them through ketchup. 'Thank you,' she said, popping the fries into her mouth and chewing, eyeing him with gratitude.

'For what?'

'For bringing me here today.' She gestured around the room. 'I needed to reconnect with my past. I just hadn't realised how much until tonight.'

'You're welcome.'

Damned if that uncomfortable ache in his chest wasn't back, as if he'd eaten too many barbecue ribs.

She glanced at him from beneath lowered lashes. 'Can I tell you something?'

'Anything.'

'Sharing this trip down memory lane has been extra special because you're here.'

That annoying ache intensified, making him want to blurt exactly how he felt. But she hadn't called him on his earlier slip-up. In fact, she couldn't have run out of the bedroom any faster if she'd tried, which told him exactly how this would go if he blabbed his true feelings.

'I've enjoyed being here.' He forced a warm smile, when in fact he wanted to haul her into his arms and bury his face in her hair.

'Okay, enough of the mushy stuff.' She snapped her fingers. 'Let's demolish this amazing food, then you can take me home.' Her eyes sparkled with enthusiasm. 'I have a very important audition to research.'

Any hope he'd harboured of spending the night withered and died right then. This was important to her. Her lifelong dream. He got it.

Didn't mean he had to like it.

CHAPTER NINETEEN

SINCE CHARLOTTE'S NEW boss had appeared on the scene, it wasn't unusual for her flatmate to stay late at work and get home around midnight. Makayla had never been gladder to have the place to herself than tonight.

Hudson had dropped her off thirty minutes ago. She'd showered, changed into her old cotton rugby jersey and sat on the sofa ever since, doing an online search for Reg Grober's upcoming shows.

The extent of Reg's backing in the theatre world blew her mind. As for the Broadway show she'd be auditioning for...if she got it, she'd be set. A major gold star on her CV. Leading to the type of roles she'd only ever dreamed about until now.

This was it.

Her big break.

So why the niggle of worry that wouldn't quit?

She knew the cause. Hudson. The guy who'd stolen her heart once before and had recaptured it a second time around.

But this time was worse, so much worse. This time,

she'd become emotionally invested to the point of envisaging him in her life every single day and he had too.

She'd been sure he'd been on the verge of blurting his feelings in her old bedroom. He'd said the L word, before masking it with some lame sidestep. And she'd been glad. Relieved. It was too much, too soon. She couldn't handle landing her dream job and dream man in the same night.

Unfortunately, the two would be mutually exclusive.

Get the job, lose the guy.

It should be a no-brainer. She'd told him right from the start that she'd never let any man jeopardise her dream. He knew the score. But outlining a bunch of clear-cut rules to continue having the best sex of her life was a far cry from falling for him and realising she couldn't have it all, no matter how much she wanted it.

A key rattled in the door a second before it opened, and Charlotte padded into the room, holding her shoes in one hand, a briefcase in the other. She jumped when she caught sight of Makayla sitting in the semi-darkness.

'Hey, everything okay?'

'Grab the wine and I'll let you know.'

'Okay.' Charlotte dumped her shoes and briefcase before heading to the kitchen. 'Though I'd rather have a hot chocolate at this time of night.'

'Make mine a double,' Makayla called out, knowing that even the smoothness of decadent chocolate wouldn't help her sleep tonight.

Her head was a spinning whirl of 'what ifs' and 'maybes' that no amount of alcohol or chocolate could dull.

'Here you go, a Charlie special with extra marshmallows.' Charlotte handed her a mug and sank into the armchair opposite.

'Charlie? I thought you hated being called that.'

'I do.' Charlotte wrinkled her nose. 'Not only is my new boss a sadistic prick who gets off by torturing me from afar with enough work for ten people, he's now taken to calling me Charlie over the phone.'

'And you put up with it?'

'I need this job.' Charlotte cradled her mug in both hands and blew on the steaming drink. 'But I promise you this. The day that the Neanderthal sets foot in the office in person is the day I accidentally on purpose drive a stake through his heart.'

Makayla laughed. 'I'd like to see that.'

'Anyway, tell me about your day and why you're out here sitting in the dark. Didn't you have a dinner date with Mr Gorgeous? I thought you'd be staying over at his place tonight.'

'Loads happened so I thought it better I sleep here tonight.'

'Uh-oh. Trouble in paradise?'

Makayla shook her head. 'Not trouble as such, more like complications.'

'Want to talk about it?' Charlotte sipped at her hot chocolate. 'I may have zero experience with men but I'm a good listener.'

Makayla didn't know where to start. So she left out the phenomenal sex-capades and the stroll down memory lane, and jumped in at the deep end.

'Hudson has used his influence in the theatre industry to get me an audition with a media mogul who needs a dancer for his latest show on Broadway.'

Charlotte almost spat her hot chocolate out. 'Really? Oh, my God, that's incredible.'

'Yeah, I know, right? I'm over the moon. Can't quite believe it, to be honest. Not that I have the gig yet, but I have a shot and that's incredible in itself.'

A frown dented Charlotte's brow. 'So what's the problem?'

Makayla cupped her hands around the mug, letting the warmth infuse her. It didn't remove the chill seeping through her bones at the thought of walking away from Hudson.

'I may have fallen for Hudson and I don't want to be in love, because it'll ruin everything I've worked so hard for. Plus I don't want to hurt him after he's been so great to me, casting me as the lead in his show here then giving me this other incredible opportunity. So I'm feeling torn between my dream and the guy, when I shouldn't be. It shouldn't be an issue. I'd usually pick the dream every time. But this is *Hudson*... argh...' She ran out of steam and slumped back in the sofa, careful not to slosh hot chocolate everywhere.

Charlotte stared at her with round eyes. 'That's some dilemma.'

'Tell me about it.' Makayla sipped at her hot chocolate. The faster she drank it, the less likelihood she'd end up wearing it if this discussion got animated. 'You're the least boy-crazy woman I know, Charlotte. You're sensible and logical and I value your unbiased opinion. So tell me what you think.'

Charlotte hesitated before placing her mug on the coffee table and resting her hands in her lap. 'Okay, but before I say anything, you know I've never had a boyfriend so maybe I'm not qualified to give any advice.' Charlotte blushed. 'I'm a sad case, I know. Still want my opinion?'

'Please. You're sensible and I need that right now.' Makayla nodded. 'You can talk me down off this ledge of my own making.'

'Well.' Charlotte blew out a breath. 'Is there a chance you can have the proverbial cake and eat it too? Get the job and the guy?'

'How? If I get the job I'll be based in New York indefinitely, which is my dream. I can't ask Hudson to wait around for me. I wouldn't do that to him.'

Charlotte frowned. 'Good point. What about a long-distance relationship?'

A flare of hope made Makayla sit up before she slumped again. 'I won't have the funds to fly back and see him once every six months and I wouldn't expect him to make all the effort, flying all that way to see me. Wouldn't be fair.' She shook her head. 'Besides, have you seen how hot he is? Could I really expect him to fend off countless women for the chance of intermittent phone sex and a face-to-face once or twice a year?'

'If he feels the same way you do, he might be interested?'

He did feel the same way and that was part of her problem. If she made it on Broadway, she didn't need the distraction of wondering if Hudson was okay with their long-distance arrangement, of how he was coping and with whom.

She'd maintained her independence until now for a reason. Nothing and no one came between her and her dream. Unfortunately, her stupid heart had betrayed her this time and she felt far more for the guy than she should.

'Sorry, sweetie, the long-distance suggestion is about as logical as I get at this time of night.' Charlotte smothered a yawn. 'Let's sleep on it and I'll let you know if I come up with anything in the morning.'

'Thanks for listening.' Mak finished off the last of her hot chocolate and stood. 'On a more practical note, you mentioned moving out a few weeks ago and our lease comes up for renewal soon. With me potentially moving, shall I inform the agent to go ahead and advertise it?'

'No. Give me a few more weeks,' Charlotte said, wrinkling her nose. 'The place I had my eye on is way more than this one and if I can't take any more of the boss's crap, I may be looking for a new job soon.'

'Okay.' Makayla hesitated, knowing her flatmate's love life was none of her business, but feeling obligated to say something. 'Don't shoot the messenger, okay? But you'll never find a boyfriend if you don't go out. Mingle. Have fun.'

'I go out,' Charlotte said, crossing her arms in classic defensive posture.

'Grocery shopping and yoga don't count.'

Charlotte poked out her tongue. 'I know you're right but I can't summon the energy to go on bad dates.

And the online sites or app thing isn't my scene.' She blushed. 'I'm not into casual hook-ups.'

Makayla covered her mouth in mock horror. 'Don't tell me you want a commitment.'

This time, Charlotte blew a raspberry. 'Something like that.'

'I'll make you a deal. Whatever happens with this audition, we'll have a girls' night out end of next week. Drag Abby along too so she's not tied to that ball and chain Tanner.'

Charlotte stared at her as if she'd proposed they trawl the streets looking for men. 'I'm not really the going-out type. I hate putting on make-up and I never have anything to wear and I don't like—'

'No excuses.' Makayla held up her hand. 'We're doing this.'

Charlotte eventually nodded. 'Fine.'

'Good.' As Makayla headed for the kitchen to rinse her mug, she paused in the doorway. 'So what would a good boyfriend entail for you? Big biceps? Big pecs? Big dick—'

The cushion Charlotte flung hit her in the head, and she laughed. 'You know, I have a feeling the right guy for you is just around the corner.'

Charlotte rolled her eyes and remained silent.

Unfortunately, Makayla had already found the right guy. She just had no idea how to hold on to him; or even if she wanted to.

CHAPTER TWENTY

HUDSON JABBED AT the punching bag over and over. Left hook. Right. Repeating the mindless exercise until sweat drenched his body and dripped into his eyes. Only then did he stop for a breather, unlacing the gloves with his teeth and tugging them off before reaching for a towel.

He swiped his face with it and draped it around his neck, taking a seat on a nearby bench while slugging water. While it quenched his thirst, it did little for the tightness in his throat. The same tightness that had plagued him since he'd blurted his feelings last night.

Even now, twenty-four hours later, he couldn't believe he'd almost told Mak he loved her. His save, 'I love…doing this,' had been lame at best. And he still had no idea if she'd bought it or not. She'd bolted so fast from the bedroom that he had an idea she hadn't.

If a woman fled after hearing that the guy she was dating loved her, it wasn't a good sign. But it had jolted him back to reality. Until that moment, he'd been living in fantasyland, thinking that Mak's enthusiasm for sex and wanting to spend time with him meant she cared.

Sadly, the only thing Mak cared about was dancing

and, while he admired her for being so invested in her work, he couldn't help but resent it.

The moment he'd told her about the Broadway audition, he'd lost her.

He'd known it would happen, which was why he'd held off so long.

What sort of asshole did that make him?

After flinging his towel away, he stretched out the kinks in his neck. It did little to ease the tension bunching his shoulder muscles. He'd thought a good workout at Jim's would soothe his frustration at a seemingly untenable situation. It hadn't.

Mak was an amazing dancer, one of the best he'd ever seen. She'd land the Broadway role and leave, nothing surer. Leaving behind the chump who'd fallen for her.

He should be happy for her. He was happy for her.

If he kept mentally reciting it long enough, he might actually believe it.

'Fuck,' he muttered, his hands unconsciously clenching into fists, and he stood, ready for another workout.

However, before he could slip his gloves back on, a kid claimed the punching bag he'd been using. A teen, about fourteen, with dyed black dreadlocks caught off his face in a headband, five piercings in each ear, another in his eyebrow and two in his lip. But that wasn't what captured Hudson's attention. The surly, defiant expression on the kid's face did.

He looked exactly how Hudson had at the same age.

Angry at the world. At the injustice of having to

take care of a drunk for a father. At the mother who'd turned her back on him.

He'd harboured that rage for a long time, until he'd learned the truth about his mum and why she'd stooped so low.

His anger towards his father still festered, which was why he made the obligatory visits as infrequent as possible. He did enough for the old bastard by placing him in a fancy special accommodation home for patients with alcohol-induced dementia and paying all his bills. That would have to do for his penance.

Hudson watched the kid for a while. His technique wasn't bad. Though he dropped his shoulders too often and his right hook needed some serious work.

He almost offered to help but one look at the feral gleam in the kid's eyes ensured he didn't move from the bench.

The kid wasn't interested in boxing skills. He needed a way to work off his antagonism at the world and every time he lay into that bag was another jab at whoever or whatever had driven him to this.

Hudson had been lucky. He'd had Tanner, who'd had an equally shitty father, and the two of them had bonded over it. They'd come down here often in their high school days, preferring to punch the crap out of a bag rather than some of the assholes at school.

Jim's had been his go-to place. His sanctuary. A world far from getting a call from the local pub to come take his dad home, from propping up the old man and half dragging him home, from dodging fists and beer bottles, from tolerating the kind of verbal abuse a kid should never have to listen to.

Hudson had resented his father to the point of hatred. He'd escaped to this gym and found solace in doing odd jobs around the Cross. Earning money had soon become his number one goal when he'd started working at thirteen, because money would be his way out. His ticket to a life far from Kings Cross and the putrid memories it held.

'Fuck this,' the kid yelled, jabbing at the bag so furiously the chain holding it bucked and rattled like a cut snake.

Still, Hudson didn't say anything, but when the kid reluctantly met his eyes, he saw every ounce of pent-up rage and sorrow and frustration he'd once harboured.

'Want a drink?' Hudson pulled another water bottle from his bag and held it out.

It didn't surprise him when the kid scowled and slouched off, skulking towards the door as if he couldn't wait to get away.

He hadn't wanted to accept help back then either. Had done his damnedest to keep people at bay. Because letting anyone get close had meant opening up about his home life and divulging secrets he hadn't wanted to reveal.

Mak had been the only person he'd allowed a small glimpse into his life. He'd trusted her, even back then. Having her back in his life had been a godsend.

Ensuring it would be all the harder when she left him.

CHAPTER TWENTY-ONE

THREE NIGHTS LATER, Mak was no closer to figuring out what to do about her relationship with Hudson. Though considering the lack of quality time they'd spent together over the last seventy-two hours, maybe they didn't even have a relationship.

For some inexplicable reason, she got the feeling he'd been avoiding her.

Usually after rehearsal she'd head to his place and they'd spend the night having wild monkey sex before sleeping curled in each other's arms. But the last three nights he'd cited work at the club that would keep him busy until the wee small hours. A perfectly reasonable explanation given he'd spent fewer hours at the club during the evenings because of her but his distinct lack of concern irked.

It was like he didn't miss her at all, when all she could think about, apart from the Grober audition tomorrow, was him.

She'd pretended his cool behaviour didn't bother her. Had been the epitome of a woman fine with a casual relationship. But he'd taken it a step further tonight when he'd yelled at her for a minor slip-up during rehearsal, and she knew she had to confront him.

Something was bugging him and she needed to find out before it ruined her concentration at the most important audition of her life.

She waited until the dancers filtered out to the dressing room before barging up to Hudson, where he propped against the bar in the corner, making notes.

'Can I talk to you for a second?'

He didn't look up and held up a finger. 'Let me finish this.'

She bit back her first retort: that it looked like he'd already finished them.

He took a full five minutes to finish scrawling and she used the time to do a few cool-down stretches while casting him surreptitious glances.

When he finally looked up and placed his clipboard down, a deep frown slashed his brow. 'You wanted to talk?'

'Is everything okay?'

Dumbass question, considering the frown and compressed lips.

'Last-minute glitches that need ironing out before opening night.' He tapped his pen against his notes. 'I should've known things wouldn't continue to unfold without a hitch.'

'Anything I can do to help?'

'Just dance your ass off on Sunday night,' he said, the frown easing slightly. 'I've been a grouchy prick and I'm sorry.'

'You don't have to apologise. Your work's important to you. I get that.'

Relieved that his funk had actually been about work and not her, she continued, 'I've got my audition for Reg tomorrow.'

'Has that come around already?' He pinched the bridge of his nose. 'Shit. I feel like I've lost days with all this work. I'm swamped.' He shook his head, as if to clear it. 'Are you ready or is that a stupid question?'

'I'm ready.'

And she meant it. She'd researched the Broadway show until her eyes ached from staring at a computer screen. In a way, not spending time with Hudson the last few days had been a godsend. She shouldn't have been so angsty about it.

'Good luck—' His cell phone rang and he fished it out of his pocket. He glanced at the screen, expression inscrutable. 'I have to take this.'

Ignoring the niggle in her gut that insisted his standoffish behaviour was more than work, she said, 'Sure, I'll go get changed and pop back in to say bye.'

He nodded absent-mindedly, already turning away to take the call. She believed in hard work but Hudson was taking it to extremes at the moment as that niggle turned into something more and she knew her acceptance of his work excuse was foolish.

He managed the hottest nightclub in Sydney. Stood to reason he'd be busy all the time, yet he'd managed to juggle hours just fine when they'd first started their hot and heavy affair. So what had happened over the last few days to change things?

Ever since their stroll down memory lane in Kings Cross he'd been distant, a palpable coolness between them.

She didn't get it.

Annoyed that she was letting her mulling ruin her concentration when she should be focussed on the all-important audition tomorrow, she grabbed her workout bag and headed for the dressing room.

However, as she neared the open door leading into the dressing room, she heard her name being mentioned so she paused.

The dance world was rife with backstage gossip. She'd lived with it ever since she'd started out in this business. Her mum had warned her about it early on, when she'd realised nothing or nobody could sway Makayla from following her dream.

For the most part, she ignored it. Bitchy backstabbing wasn't her thing. But as she heard one of the male dancers call her a snooty bitch, she edged closer to the doorway. Eavesdropping wasn't her style either but she didn't want anything jeopardising Hudson's show, considering he had to make it fly.

'Did you hear the way he yelled at Miss Bossy Boots today? About time the big guy ripped those sex blinkers from his eyes and took her down a notch or two.'

Bossy Boots? As lead dancer she had the authority to discuss moves with her fellow dancers. Did that make her bossy? She'd wear it.

But sex blinkers? Her blood chilled. If they thought Hudson wore sex blinkers where she was concerned…

how did they know? Hell. She'd made it clear to Hudson at the start that no one could find out about them for this very reason.

'Probably the only way she scored lead dancer,' a higher-pitched voice piped up. 'Sleeping with the boss is a sure-fire way to score the top job, even if you're an average performer.'

If her blood had frozen a few moments ago, it positively boiled now. Her secret was out and had resulted in exactly what she'd hoped to avoid. Innuendo.

And average? That was a low blow. She might not have an ego the size of the Opera House but she knew she was a damn sight better than average.

'You sure she's sleeping with him?' A third voice, a baritone of one of the other male dancers, chimed in. 'They don't appear all that close at rehearsals.'

The woman snickered. 'Are you blind? The way they look at each other when they think no one's looking is positively sickening. They're definitely bumping uglies.'

'Gross,' the baritone said. 'Doesn't mean she got the lead that way.'

'You're dumb as well as having two left feet,' the other guy said. 'I know for a fact my friend Sha auditioned for the lead and didn't even end up alongside us in the chorus, so the redhead definitely got her shot by bonking the boss.'

'You're wrong,' the baritone insisted. 'She's amazing. I've worked in stage shows all around Australia, as well as London and Paris, and I haven't seen a lead dancer as good as her.'

Makayla had to clamp down on the urge to barge in there and kiss the guy.

'You're all just jealous so, instead of moaning and bitching, why don't you all pull your fingers out and step up?' He paused and Makayla held her breath, wondering what her knight in shining armour would say next. 'I love dancing but I hate this industry because of moronic, narrow-minded idiots like all of you.'

Makayla wanted to applaud so badly she curled her fingers into fists to refrain.

Silence followed her defender's proclamation, before the woman finally spoke. 'You're right. I'm jealous as hell she's so damn good. She makes every routine look effortless and I hate her for that.'

The guy whose friend Sha missed out on being cast in the show said, 'I still think she shagged the boss to get the role.'

Makayla didn't wait around to hear any more.

She had to confront Hudson and discover why he'd opened his big mouth.

That was when realisation hit. Was that why he'd been avoiding her the last few days? Was he feeling guilty for letting slip their secret? Had it been a mistake or had he hoped to rattle her into admitting they had more than a casual thing and had moved into serious relationship territory?

If so, he was in for a rude shock.

She wouldn't be pushed into anything, least of all a relationship that could derail her lifelong plans.

CHAPTER TWENTY-TWO

HUDSON SLIPPED HIS cell back into his pocket and stared aimlessly at the vacated stage.

He hated confrontation and would do anything to avoid it. Even as a kid he'd hide under his bed when he heard his father stumble in, bumping into walls and swearing vociferously, to avoid the inevitable skirmish that would take place.

At school, he'd used words rather than fists to work off his frustrations, and had taught Tanner to do the same.

Working odd jobs in Kings Cross as a teen had taught him the best life lesson to avoid confrontation: know how to read people. He'd been honest, savvy and dedicated to getting a job done, three qualities most people admired.

He saw those qualities in Mak and his admiration for her knew no bounds.

Now he had to be the one to tear her dream down.

'Fuck,' he muttered, dragging his hand through his hair.

Reg Grober had called, doing him the courtesy of letting him know first that the producer in New York had already filled the dance slot. Which meant Mak would be getting a call from Reg's casting agency soon.

He'd asked Reg to give him half an hour before the agency called, as he wanted to be the one to tell her. He felt bad enough about how he'd been treating her the last few days, it seemed only right.

Because establishing emotional distance between them before their impending break-up was a hell of a lot easier in theory than in practice. It had killed him, watching her walk out of rehearsal each evening, knowing he'd chosen to let her go rather than take her home to his bed and ravish her.

But he'd had to do it, had to put himself through the torture of weaning himself off her rather than going cold turkey when she left.

Now, he felt stupid. Her audition had fallen through, which meant she wouldn't be jetting off to New York soon. She'd be disappointed but he couldn't help but feel relieved.

Mak would be sticking around. And that meant… what?

They could continue deepening their relationship, only for her to eventually leave anyway?

They could maintain the status quo, both ignoring the obvious—that they were in way deeper than they thought?

They could pretend that being emotionally invested in a relationship that had no future wasn't the dumbest thing either of them had ever done?

Before he could mentally rehearse a way of letting her down gently, Mak stormed into the room and slammed the door shut behind her.

'Why did you do it?' She stalked towards him, her hands balled into fists and resting on her hips. 'Do you have any idea how this undermines me?'

Confused, Hudson stared at five-ten of angry woman advancing on him. Had the agency already rung her and she thought he'd had something to do with the audition being cancelled? If so, it revealed what she really thought of him and it wasn't good.

'Look, I had nothing to do with—'

'Don't make this worse by lying,' she said through gritted teeth. 'Do you think I'm an idiot? How else would they have found out?'

Okay, so this wasn't about the audition. It didn't make him feel any better considering she now stood close enough to jab him in the chest, fury radiating off her, making the fine hairs at her temples stand out as if she'd stuck her finger in a power socket.

'You knew when we started up that I didn't want people to know about us. You knew!' Her chest heaved as she sucked in breaths to calm her anger. He shouldn't have been turned on, but he was. It made him feel even worse. 'Now they're saying exactly what I thought they'd say if they found out—that the only way I got the lead role was by sleeping with the boss.'

'Mak—'

'Why can't guys ever keep their big mouths shut?'

He'd been about to placate her but that jibe, lumping him with the rest of the guys she'd been with, stung.

'I didn't say a word to anyone about us,' he said,

sounding lethally calm when in fact he wanted to yell at her for not trusting him enough. 'I wouldn't do that to you and it'd be nice if you thought I was a good guy who wouldn't betray you like that.'

Some of her anger deflated as her shoulders sagged. 'It mightn't have been intentional. You might've been swapping locker-room talk with Tanner and maybe someone overheard—'

'I didn't do this, Mak.'

Shit, if she was pissed at him about this, wait until he delivered the really bad news.

He could couch it in fancy terms, try to let her down gently, but he was seriously annoyed she thought he was a prick who'd talk about their relationship to others when she'd specifically asked him not to.

He'd give it to her straight.

'While you're hell-bent on blaming me for stuff I didn't do, I've got more bad news.'

Her lips compressed into a thin, unimpressed line as she glared at him in condemnation. Her frosty silence spoke volumes. Sadly, it reminded him of the last time they'd had a major blowout five years earlier, when he'd hurled vile accusations at her and she'd done nothing but stand there and take it.

He'd wanted her to defend herself, to tell him he was wrong in assuming she'd chosen a life that could only end in pain. But she'd clammed up, staring at him with such hatred he'd had no option but to leave.

He hoped this time it wouldn't mean the end of them too.

'That call I just took? Reg Grober doing me the

courtesy of letting me know that the audition for the Broadway show is off. The producer in New York found someone.'

Mak's jaw dropped and she stared at him in disbelief. 'What the hell?'

'It's showbiz. It happens.' He shrugged, knowing he'd made a major mistake when she blanched and took a step back.

'It *happens*?' she mimicked, her eyes spitting so much fire he should've been fried on the spot. 'Could you be any more dismissive of my dream?'

'I feel bad for you but you'd be used to disappointment in the industry—'

'Shut the fuck up!' Disgust twisted her features as she strode towards the door, leaving him gobsmacked.

He'd expected disappointment.

He hadn't expected this level of rage.

Like she blamed him somehow.

When she stopped at the door and placed her palms against it, bracing, with her head hanging, he wanted to go to her.

He didn't.

Because he'd seen this kind of irrational anger before, when the seething person needed a scapegoat. He'd done it often enough with his dad in the past to know he wouldn't put up with it again, even from the woman he loved.

So he stood there. Watching. Waiting. Knowing without a shadow of a doubt that when she turned around and spoke, they'd be over.

CHAPTER TWENTY-THREE

MAKAYLA'S CHEST BURNED with the effort of holding back tears. She'd come in here spoiling for a fight, wanting to hurt Hudson as much as he'd hurt her by revealing their secret.

Then he'd gone and denied it, his honesty evident in his guileless eyes, and she'd felt like the biggest bitch in the world.

Until he'd lumped more crap on her and while she leaned against the door, trying to reassemble her wits, she couldn't deny the one prominent thought front and centre in her head.

That he didn't seem to care her dream had been shattered.

In fact, that aggravating shrug indicated complete nonchalance. A real 'shit happens' moment. And the anger she'd struggled to contain bubbled up again, swamping her in wave after wave of rage until she shook with it.

Spinning back around, she tried to calm herself. Failed. Deep down she knew that until she purged her innermost, insidious thoughts, she'd feel this crappy for a while.

'You're happy about this, aren't you?' She took small, measured steps towards him until they were two feet apart. Within slugging distance, not the best thought at a time like this. 'I get to stay in Sydney and we continue this thing between us. Is that it?'

'You're disappointed, I get it. But don't shoot the messenger.' His expression grim, he held up his hands. Yeah, like that would calm her. 'The agency would've called you direct about cancelling but because I put your name forward to Reg personally, he did me the courtesy of calling first. And I asked him to give me half an hour so I could tell you myself.'

'I suppose I should be grateful for that,' she said, sounding childish and churlish and hating herself for it. 'But whichever way you dress this up, whoever delivers the news, it's still the same. It sucks.'

This time when he shrugged, she had to use every ounce of self-control not to knock him on his ass.

'There'll be other opportunities. Other auditions—'

'For Broadway? Unlikely.' She shook her head, wishing he understood how momentous this had been for her. 'You think I'm being irrational and over the top but this is my life. Don't you get that?'

He didn't make a move to comfort her. Didn't move a muscle. He just stood there, way too calm, way too controlled. Like a freaking robot.

'I get it.'

When he finally spoke, his low lethal tone raised goosebumps on her arms.

'I get that losing out on this one audition has sent you into such a tailspin you seem to be blaming me for it. I get that the thought of sticking around and having a relationship with me is seemingly abhorrent to you.' His tone didn't change but his eyes…his eyes turned a glacial blue that sent a shiver through her. 'I get that maybe I was just a means to an end for you. That you used me to get the big break you've always wanted. That I mean nothing to you.'

He flung the hurtful accusations in her face clearly and concisely, each hitting home like a poison-tipped dart.

She hadn't used him.

Had she?

This was Hudson, the guy she'd fantasised about as a teen. The guy who'd stood by her. The guy who'd left because of his own demons.

Ironic, that this time she'd be the one to end things between them. Not as payback, but as a way of assuming the control she didn't have last time.

She'd still hurt. A thousand times worse this time, considering she'd fallen for him. But at least she wouldn't be left feeling as if he'd never given her a chance.

This time, they'd taken that chance.

And failed.

'If you truly believe all that BS you just spouted at me, you're delusional. I don't know what happened here tonight. I don't know if the audition being cancelled was fate or you using any means possible to keep me around or just more of my crappy luck, but

I'm done waiting for my big break.' She tapped her chest. '*I'm* going to make it happen.'

Bitterness bracketed his mouth. 'You're still accusing me of being underhanded to maintain our status quo?' He barked out a laugh devoid of amusement. 'You really think I'm a shit, don't you?'

She almost reached for him then, the bewilderment tinged with hurt on his face was that heart wrenching.

But she couldn't back down now. She had to follow through.

She was done depending on others, particularly Hudson, for her happiness.

'Once your show is done, I'm heading to New York.' She squared her shoulders, the idea sounding less ludicrous articulated out loud. 'I'm going to make it on my own, without help from anyone.'

Shock made his pupils dilate, eclipsing all that beautiful blue she'd miss so much. 'So that's it? You're just going to head to the States with no job, no work permit and limited funds?' Scepticism pinched his mouth. 'How are you going to survive 'til you land your big break?'

He stared fixedly at some point over her shoulder, unable to meet her eyes, and in that moment she knew what had him so angsty. She just knew, deep down in that part of her that could never turn back time and change her decision.

Not that she would. She'd stripped that one night to honour her mum, to thank her for the many years of sacrifice, to give her the send-off she deserved.

Hudson knew that now yet he still didn't trust her

enough. He didn't believe in her, that she could survive without spiralling into some seedy way of life he obviously abhorred.

She tapped her bottom lip, pretending to think, before snapping her fingers. 'I know. If I can't make ends meet I can always take off my clothes for money. Or even better, become an escort. Or something equally nefarious that you seem to think I'm one step away from.'

'Don't be ridiculous,' he snapped, but the spots of high colour on his cheekbones belied his denial. 'I'm just worried about you—'

'I'm a big girl. I can take care of myself.' Hurting all the way to her soul, she made a grand show of glancing at her watch. 'Better head home and start making travel plans. I'll see you at final rehearsal tomorrow.'

She wanted him to say something, anything, to make her stay.

She wanted some kind of sign that they weren't over, that there was the faintest hope they could still make this work somehow.

She wanted it all: Broadway, stardom, him.

Sadly, Makayla had learned a long time ago that what she wanted and what she got were poles apart.

Her heart broke anew as Hudson just stood there, radiating disapproval, a frown creasing his brow, as he watched her back towards the door, where she spun around and marched through it, head held high.

CHAPTER TWENTY-FOUR

AS IF HUDSON'S shitty week couldn't get any worse, he'd received a call from his father's special accommodation facility first thing this morning, asking him to come in. The nurse hadn't specified the problem exactly but had forcefully suggested he pay a visit today.

This after the blow-up with Mak last night and a maximum of ninety minutes' sleep when he'd finally made it home from work at four a.m.

He'd thought discovering her naked on stage that night years ago had been bad. It had nothing on the way they'd imploded last night.

The way she'd confronted him, not giving him a chance to explain, thinking the worst of him…he'd had that a lot growing up. Teachers not believing in him because of his home life. Friends judging him for not having a good enough home to invite them over to hang out. Bosses not trusting him because nobody trusted anyone in the Cross, until he proved himself many times over.

That lack of belief drove him to be the best. To show the world that no matter what hardships he faced as a kid, nothing or nobody could keep him down. He prided himself on his work ethic, his dependability, his honesty.

Apparently, it all meant jack to Mak.

He'd been wise to distance himself this week, to re-erect emotional barriers. Their relationship had ended as he'd expected. Well, not quite what he'd expected. He'd envisaged them staying friends. Good friends. The kind of friends who chatted regularly and did video conferencing and even hopped on a plane to New York if the impulse hit.

Who was he kidding? He'd hoped they could've been a hell of a lot more than friends but that had been shot to shit.

He was better off without her.

Then why did he feel so goddamn bad?

Pulling into the parking lot of the special accommodation home, he killed the engine. It usually took him a few moments of gaining composure before he could face his father. It was the same every time he visited. Too much had happened between them, too many bad memories, to forget.

He'd tried. Had gone through a rough patch when he'd hit eighteen and gone in search of his mum. What he'd learned had driven him to drink, spending night after night drowning his sorrows in a bottle. Until he'd taken one look in the mirror, seen the resemblance to dear old dad and snapped out of it, switching to OJ without the vodka.

He'd confronted his father with the truth. Had blamed him for everything. Predictably, his old man hadn't given a shit. Had called his mother every name under the sun and accused her of driving him to drink.

Hudson knew better.

He knew the real culprit in his disastrous upbringing and it sure as hell wasn't his mother.

Taking a deep breath, he blew it out, counted to ten and opened the car door. The first thing to hit him was the sea air. Tangy. Stringent. The second thing was the views. The endless expanse of Sydney Harbour, a perfect cerulean today, dotted with sailboats and yachts, with mansions scattering north shore in the distance.

Though his father didn't deserve it he'd chosen one of the nicest accommodations in the city and paid the exorbitant rates for the privilege. Tanner accused him of being a soft touch with a core of marshmallow and his friend was probably right. But the moment he'd set foot in this place after checking out six other dementia homes, he'd known this was the right one.

Maybe it was sentimentality, maybe it was guilt, or maybe it was a futile wish he could've done something like this for his mum; whatever it was, he'd handed over the hefty entry fee for his father and worked his ass off to keep paying the bills.

If there was such a thing as karma he'd be in line for a whole heap of good stuff coming his way. Though if that were the case, his relationship with Mak would've worked out.

Swiping a hand over his face, he slammed the car door, stabbed at the remote to lock it and strode towards the front doors. Perfectly manicured lawns flanked the terracotta-bricked path, wide enough to fit two wheelchairs side by side. Flower beds filled with a riot of colour edged the garden, with towering eucalypts casting shade over the lawns.

The entire scene screamed peaceful and he absorbed as much of the ambience as he could before the upcoming confrontation. He needed it, because his obligatory visits to his father only went two ways. His father having lucid moments where he'd berate him for locking him away in this 'jail' or a bad day, where the dementia would make him ramble, alternating between angry and recalcitrant. Exactly how he'd been as a mean drunk.

Hudson didn't visit often. He felt he'd paid his dues by keeping his father at home for as long as he had and now, with this luxury accommodation. But being summoned by the nurses couldn't be a good thing and he braced himself for what he'd find.

Squaring his shoulders, he strode up the front steps and the glass doors slid open soundlessly. The faintest waft of lavender filled the foyer, probably filtered through the air conditioning ducts to calm the residents. A gleaming mahogany front desk, reminiscent of a five-star hotel, ran the length of the foyer, with huge floral arrangements strategically placed at either end.

The place definitely had a hotel feel; until he stepped through the electronically locked doors and realised his father's mind had deteriorated to the point he had to be confined.

Fixing a smile on his face, he approached the front desk. 'Hudson Watt to see Wiley Watt, my father.'

He didn't recognise the forty-something receptionist. Then again, considering his infrequent visits, it wasn't unusual.

She smiled and pointed at the locked door. 'Go right ahead. I'll buzz you in.'

When he had his hand on the handle, she said, 'You have the same eyes as Wiley.'

Blurry and nasty? He hoped not. He managed a terse nod and pushed open the door when it buzzed.

The lavender scent was stronger here, as if the cleaners were trying to drown out the smells of antiseptic and old people. It made his nose twitch.

The nurses' station stood just inside the door, a central rotund area that resembled a high-tech spaceship. Its positioning gave the nurses full view of every room and every corridor leading to the rec rooms, the grounds and the dining area. Perfect for occupants with a tendency to wander.

He recognised several of the nurses, particularly the younger ones who never failed to flirt with him. But his heart wasn't in it today so he offered them a grim smile before turning his attention to the matron who'd called him.

'Thanks for coming, Hudson.' She folded her arms, a defensive posture that wasn't a good sign.

'How's Wiley?'

He never called him Dad any more. Wiley Watt didn't deserve the title.

'He's been asking for you a lot lately. That's why I called.' She paused, as if searching for the right words. 'He's due for his annual check-up and we'll wait to see what the doctor says, but the dementia seems to be worsening. Most of his ramblings centre on you and a woman I assume is your mother, Kim? It makes him very upset. To the point he cries.'

Hudson's heart turned over. Bit late for dear old dad to grow a conscience. 'Is he lucid today?'

She nodded. 'It's one of his better days, which is why I thought you should come in and have a chat to him. See if he can make peace with whatever is bugging him so he'll be more subdued on other days?'

She didn't need to spell it out. His dad must've been saying some pretty revealing, damning stuff during his demented ramblings and the nurses thought that talking to him might ease the guilt. As if. Wiley Watt would need a year's worth of confessionals to bring some semblance of peace.

'I'll talk to him,' he said, sounding like he'd rather have a root canal. 'Thanks for letting me know.'

The nurse hesitated, before briefly touching his arm. 'I've worked in dementia wards for twenty-six years and it's rare to see people exhibit the level of regret your father is showing because they can't usually process emotions for events in the past, particularly when alcohol is the precipitating cause of the dementia. So give him a chance, okay?'

Hudson couldn't promise anything so remained silent.

The nurse sighed, her lack of judgement appreciated. 'He's in his room.'

'Thanks.'

Nothing his father could say would change the devastation of the past but if it made the nurses' jobs easier he'd listen to whatever the old man had to say.

The ten steps from the nurses' station to his father's room always seemed to take an eternity, as if his feet refused to move and dragged across the pristine carpet.

He knocked at the door, waited the obligatory five seconds, before opening it and entering. He'd learned early on during his visits that his father never answered his door and if he waited for him to open it he'd be here all day.

Wiley sat in a recliner armchair next to a large window, sunlight streaming through and warming him like a cat, bald head gleaming. For someone who'd imbibed enough alcohol in his lifetime to pickle his liver and his brain, he didn't look too bad. Wrinkles crisscrossed his face, set in a perpetual dour expression, but he maintained a good bodyweight. He appeared fit for his seventy-eight years. If not for the dementia, Wiley would still probably be drinking himself to sleep every day.

Like every other visit, Wiley ignored him until Hudson sat in a chair opposite him. 'Hey.'

'What are you doing here?' The same guttural tone, almost a snarl, that Hudson had endured every day growing up.

'Came to see how you're doing.'

'I'm locked away in a loony bin full of stinking old fools, how do you think I'm doing?'

So he was having a good day. Completely lucid. Hudson didn't know if that boded well or not.

'This is a good place. You're well looked after,' he

said, wishing he could rattle the selfish old goat and make him understand exactly how hard he had to work to pay the bills.

'You still working odd jobs at the Cross?'

Wiley's question came out of left field. In all the years he'd been here he'd never asked anything about Hudson's job, let alone the jobs he'd worked as a teen to keep food on the table.

'No, I manage a nightclub now. And I'm involved in theatre.'

Wiley screwed up his nose and snorted. 'Pansy-ass occupations, if you ask me.'

'I didn't.'

Hudson waited, curious to see what else his father would say and more than a little hopeful he'd reveal more about his mother.

He'd never forget the day he'd found her. Far too late. It had haunted him ever since.

He'd wanted to know more about the mother he remembered as a toddler, the mother who'd cuddled him every chance she could, the mother who'd smelled like exotic frangipanis, the mother who'd tell him bedtime stories and tuck him in every night.

That was the woman he wanted to remember, not the woman lying in a grimy bedsit with a needle sticking out of her arm.

'Your mother wanted you to be a lawyer.'

Hudson startled. As if Wiley had read his mind, he'd mentioned his mum.

'Bloodsucking leeches, the lot of 'em, but would've paid well.' Wiley ran a hand over his head, smoothing back non-existent hair. 'She was dating one when we met. But couldn't resist my charms so we got hitched three months later.'

Hudson couldn't imagine his father having a single charming bone in his selfish body but he remained silent.

'I've been thinking a lot about her lately. When I'm not…' Wiley made loopy circles at his temple. 'Hate how I can't bloody remember my own name half the time.'

Another first, Wiley admitting he had a problem with his memory.

'Docs say the alcohol did it.' Wiley shook his head, having the guts to look guilty for once. 'Looks like the alcohol did a lot of things to screw up my life back then.'

His father didn't deserve an ounce of pity but for a moment, Hudson felt something close to it. 'You could've stopped at any time.'

How many times had he tipped bottles down the sink in the hope his dad would stop drinking? How many times had he heard Wiley's empty promises that he wouldn't touch another drop of the demon drink? How many times had he propped him up on the way home from the pub despite Wiley saying he'd only popped in for lemonade?

Empty promises to match his empty life since his mum had left him to be raised by a mean prick.

'I only drank to stop the pain here.' Wiley thumped a fist over his heart. 'Kim broke it when she left.'

He lowered his hand, shaking slightly. 'My fault.

I drove her away. Was never good enough for her, made her do terrible things for the money then hated her for it…'

Hudson knew his mother had turned to prostitution to survive. The woman who'd owned the bedsit had told him more than he'd wanted to know and then some when he'd tracked down his mum in Melbourne and found her dead.

But never in his worst nightmares had he suspected Wiley had made her do it while they were married.

'What did you make her do?' He spoke with lethal precision, using every ounce of self-control not to pummel this shell of a man who'd never done a single thing to earn the title of father.

'I was working full time as a mechanic when we met. We got married fast, had you nine months later so she gave up her teaching degree. But I couldn't cope with a baby, was a lousy father.' Wiley coughed and Hudson waited. He hadn't known any of this.

From the time he was old enough to understand anything, his father hadn't worked. He'd sat around the house, drinking, a belligerent man who'd scared the bejesus out of him. His mum had been the one to go out and work, mainly nights. Those had been the pits, when he'd be left with an angry man he barely knew who'd yell at him to stay in his room and not come out.

Some nights he'd gone to bed hungry, wishing his mum would suddenly appear like a guardian angel. But he'd be asleep by the time she came home and he'd fling himself into her arms first thing in the morning, not breathing a word of how terrified he was of his father.

'I couldn't work with a hangover so after you were a few months old I lost my job. That's when things got tough.' Wiley glared at him as if it were his fault. 'Kim had no qualifications so she took whatever jobs she could. Check-out chick. Cleaner. Waitress. It still wasn't enough.'

Sorrow made Wiley's eyelids droop and for a moment Hudson thought he'd fallen asleep.

'A friend told me how much she could make in the strip clubs, taking her clothes off. I encouraged Kim to do it because we needed the money desperately.' Wiley's upper lip curled in disgust and Hudson didn't know if it was at the thought of Kim stripping or at himself for pushing her into it. 'It took the pressure off. The money was a godsend. But I couldn't look at her the same way.'

Wiley blinked rapidly, and Hudson hoped to God he wouldn't start crying. What he was hearing made him sick to his stomach. He didn't want to cope with crocodile tears too.

'Made the mistake of going to a club to watch one night. And that was the end of it for me. I snapped.' Wiley pressed his fingertips to his eyes. Hudson resisted the urge to do the same. 'Said I couldn't come near her again. That what we had was over. Drove her away deliberately with day after day of abuse.' Wiley waved his arm around. 'And ended up here because of it, a lonely old man losing his mind.'

Impotent rage simmered in Hudson's gut, a slow-burning anger he'd harboured against his father for years. The old bastard deserved it, considering he'd driven his mother away because of something he'd pushed her into doing in the first place.

But no one had held a gun to his mum's head once she'd established distance. She could've found another job, could've come for him and taken him away from his drunkard, pathetic excuse for a father.

Instead, she'd followed the money and taken the step from stripping to prostitution. And she hadn't looked back. Hadn't called him. Hadn't come for him.

The kicker? He could identify with what his father had felt the night he'd seen Kim stripping, because he'd felt the same way when he'd seen Mak naked on stage. It had changed everything between them. He'd been angry too and he'd taken it out on her, driving a wedge between their friendship for years.

The only way he'd found his way back to her was once he'd learned the truth about her motivations. That was where he differed from Wiley. He'd known Kim's motivations but he'd lashed out anyway. Bastard.

'Why are you telling me all this now?'

Wiley slumped further into the chair, as if he was trying to disappear into it. 'Because I was a shit husband and a shit father and I don't want to go to my grave without telling you the truth.'

'That you were a mean-spirited drunk who pushed my mother away and left me being the primary caregiver for you?'

Wiley shrugged, as if the years of Hudson's sacrifice and hard work meant little.

'Been having a lot of dreams lately. Nightmares. Past blending into the present, that kind of thing.' Wiley plucked at a thread in the seam of his corduroys. 'Just felt like I had to tell someone.'

'Lucky me,' Hudson muttered. He'd heard enough. He felt pity for his father, for the shell of a man he'd become. But he couldn't forgive him. The time for absolution had long passed.

'What are you doing here? Get out of my room!' Wiley bellowed, pushing to his feet with difficulty and brandishing a non-existent cane. 'I don't let strangers into my room. Nurse!'

Hudson stood and headed for the door, relieved to leave. The switch from lucid to confusion happened like this sometimes, so quickly he didn't have time to come up with a way to placate his irate dad.

'Get out, I said.' His father's face turned puce, the familiar colour of anger Hudson recognised well from the old days. 'Get out!'

Hudson did exactly that, without a backward glance.

CHAPTER TWENTY-FIVE

MAKAYLA LOVED THE thrill of opening night. The anticipation of performing in front of a crowd. The culmination of many hours of rehearsal. The smell of make-up and hairspray mingling with the sweat of nerves. The excited chatter of performers about to strut their stuff. She'd been doing this for years and it never got old.

But this opening night didn't hold her enthralled like others.

Because once this opening night concluded, she only had another nine shows at Embue until she left her old life behind and embarked on her new one.

She'd had three days to scrounge together the money to book flights, organise travel documents and find short-term accommodation. She'd been lucky, using a contact in the industry to gain a working permit and scoring a room in a brownstone shared by four other wannabe dancers. So once her commitment at Embue was done, she'd be leaving.

She should be ecstatic.

So why the lethargy that wouldn't quit?

She'd managed to get through the remaining rehearsals by feigning complete indifference towards Hudson and he'd done the same, treating her with a frosty politeness that made her yearn for their old warmth.

But their friendship was ruined along with any chance they might have had at maintaining something more. She should've been relieved. It would've been a struggle, doing the long-distance thing. Yet seeing Hudson the past three days and not being able to tease or laugh or smile at him had been torture.

Her fingers had itched to run through his artfully mussed dark blond hair. Her eyes had automatically sought his, searching for some kind of emotion in that unique indigo blue. Her body had yearned to be close to him, to feel the heat, the spark that never failed to ignite her in a way that would never be replicated by any other man.

That was another thing. Now that she'd had phenomenally great sex, how could she ever settle for anything less? The whole situation was beyond annoying. Maybe the first thing she did when she landed in the States was find the hottest American she could and shag him senseless?

Yeah, and if it were that easy, she would've been having great sex for years. Instead, the hotties were too egotistical and lazy in bed, while the nice guys with a modicum of talent didn't do it for her outside the bedroom.

Hudson had been the best of both worlds. Worlds that had well and truly collided and imploded.

'Damn it,' she muttered, the outer corner of her fake eyelashes slipping a tad as she tried to glue it.

Mulling about the past wasn't conducive to kicking ass on stage and she wanted to do a good job if it killed her. She had to prove to Hudson that their break up didn't affect her at all. Even if her hands shook and her legs wobbled at the thought of dancing on stage in front of him.

Last time he'd seen her on stage that hadn't involved rehearsals it hadn't ended well. The thing was, that night haunted her more than it must've ever bugged him.

She'd moved past the shame but she'd never been able to shake the deep-seated belief that there might've been another way to get the money she'd needed for her mum's funeral.

A sharp knock sounded at the door before Hudson stuck his head around it. 'Ready?'

She nodded, not willing to answer when her voice might quiver as badly as her insides.

He paused, as if wanting to say something else, before half shrugging. 'On stage in ten.'

When he left, she exhaled a breath she hadn't been aware she'd been holding. Ten minutes to pull herself together.

And nail this performance.

She went through her routine pre-performance stretches and, after a final glance in the mirror, made her way backstage with a minute to spare. The other dancers milled around, going through their individual pre-performance superstitions. Some touched the curtains. Some tucked a lucky talisman into a secure place. Some did deep breathing, eyes closed.

Makayla had never believed in luck. She made her own. Starting now.

As Hudson did the intro and the curtain rose, she strutted onto the stage for the opening number.

And stumbled.

It hadn't happened once in rehearsals and it momentarily threw her. Thankfully, the other dancers were out on stage quickly, doing their own spins and pirouettes and shimmies.

Makayla had faced other minor mishaps on stage before. All part of the biz. But for some reason, she didn't recover from that initial stumble and for the next forty minutes, she struggled.

Missed steps by a beat. Felt stiff and uncoordinated. Lacked her usual joy for dance. And it must've showed. She only risked a glance at Hudson in the wings once and his stony expression told her everything she already knew.

She stank.

Mortified, she managed the finale before limping off stage, her Achilles aching as much as her pride.

She went through the routine of backslapping fellow dancers and feigning enthusiasm, all the while wishing she could sink into the floor. After that pathetic performance, she would've cemented what they already suspected: that the only way she'd got the lead role was by sleeping with the boss. Ugh.

Slipping away from the mini celebration as quickly

as possible, she headed for her dressing room. The sooner she got the hell out of here, the better.

She'd planned on rubbing Hudson's nose in it, triumphant in her professionalism. Instead, she'd let her earlier musings derail her and had put in the worst performance of her entire career.

Not waiting to remove her make-up or change out of costume, she slipped on an overcoat, grabbed her bag and made a run for it.

CHAPTER TWENTY-SIX

HUDSON WATCHED THE dancers mill about backstage. He should be mingling out front of the house, where enthusiastic patrons raved about the show while spending big at the bar.

But he couldn't tear his eyes away from Mak.

She looked...broken.

As if all the spirit had drained out of her.

Sure, she'd given a lacklustre performance but only an industry expert could tell. The audience had still applauded every move and clapped madly at the end when she'd taken the final bow.

But she'd been seriously rattled after that initial stumble and hadn't recovered. It surprised him, because she'd been flawless at rehearsals.

Unless...he'd never seen her perform in a show on stage. Was she one of those dancers who nailed the previews but couldn't translate it on the big stage?

He'd seen it before, actors who memorised entire scripts but couldn't enunciate a word in front of a crowd. Singers who performed in pubs but lost their pitch when they got their big break.

Was Mak a choker when it really counted?

He hated to think it. Followed by another worrying thought. If tonight's performance was anything to go by, how did she expect to make it on Broadway?

She'd be wasting her time, going from audition to audition, her funds dwindling. What would she do then?

The memory of her stripping naked on stage popped into his head. Fuck. Would she return to that in the US? Or like his mum, desperate for cash, much worse?

He knew nothing about her financial situation beyond what she'd told him: that she had a flatmate because her part-time job at Le Miel couldn't cover the bills alone. She might have savings but if so, why hadn't she chosen to head to the States before now…? Damn.

He watched her slip away from the dancers, was about to follow her, when a hand landed on his shoulder.

'Good work, bozo.' Tanner squeezed his shoulder, then released him. 'You may be onto something with these live dance shows.'

'Thanks.' Hudson's gaze didn't leave Mak, wishing she'd glance over her shoulder so he could signal to her to wait for him.

'If you pack the crowd in like this over the next two weeks, I may need to think about making this a permanent gig.' Tanner slapped him on the back. 'And give you a raise.'

Another back slap and Tanner was gone, leaving Hudson craning his neck looking for Mak. She'd vanished.

Cursing under his breath, he headed for her dressing room, bypassing the dancers who'd waylay him. He should be with them, congratulating and encouraging. Yet all he could think about was getting to Mak.

The desperate edge to his urgency scared him. For someone who'd ended their relationship without a backward glance, he sure was concerned about her. In fact, it was more than concern. It was an ache in his gut that screamed…fear.

The abject failure he'd seen on Mak's face terrified him.

He didn't want her feeling like that. He wanted to pick her up and cradle her and tell her how frigging fantastic she was.

He wouldn't put her down or push her away when she needed him most.

He wasn't his father.

In that moment, he realised something else. He didn't want to be alone like Wiley either. He didn't want to live with regrets or end up by himself in some old-age home because he hadn't taken a chance on love.

He wouldn't hold Mak back but he wouldn't let her go either.

He'd fight.

Make a stand.

As he should have that night he'd seen her strip and given up on her.

Who knew, dear old dad had done him a favour, revealing the truth about what happened with his mum.

Wiley had been a quitter.

Luckily, Hudson was nothing like his father.

CHAPTER TWENTY-SEVEN

MAKAYLA HAD ALMOST made it to her car in the staff underground parking lot when Hudson burst out of a side door.

Damn it, the one person she'd hoped to avoid. She could pretend she hadn't seen him and get into her car as fast as humanly possible, but that would be poor form considering he'd given her this job at a time she'd needed it most.

She waited until he got closer, feigning nonchalance by leaning against the open driver's door. 'Is there a problem?'

'You tell me,' he said, sounding frantic, his words clipped, his voice just above a growl. 'It's usual to have a debrief after the first performance but you bolted out of there.'

'I'm exhausted.'

The lie slipped easily from her lips and she threw her bag onto the back seat in an effort to hasten her exit. 'Can we do the debrief tomorrow?'

'No.'

He took a step closer, invading her personal space

in a way she would've loved last week. Now, not so much. The tantalising fragrance of his crisp aftershave reminded her of how he smelled delicious, all over, and how much she was missing out on by not having him in her life any more.

'Hudson, I'm not in the mood—'

'What happened in there?' He jerked a thumb over his shoulder towards the club. As if she needed the clarification. She knew exactly what he was talking about. 'Not that the audience noticed, but I did.'

Hating that she'd need to have the conversation she'd hoped to avoid, she shrugged. 'You of all people know it's been a big week. Plenty of upheaval.' She tapped her head. 'All the crap up here affected my performance tonight. It won't happen again.'

His eyes narrowed. 'So that's all it was? Opening night nerves? Over-analysing?'

She hadn't been talking about the dancing and he knew it. But she was all for wrapping this up as soon as possible and leaving.

'I've never danced the lead role before. And I'm ashamed to say it rattled me tonight. That's it.'

'Are you sure?'

Another step forward, bringing him within touching distance, and she had to curl her fingers into her palms to stop from doing just that.

'Because as I recall, most of that *upheaval* had to do with you and me. And you having to travel to the other side of the world to avoid having the kind of conversation we're about to have.'

A nervous fluttering started deep in Makayla's belly

and wouldn't let up. She didn't want to have any conversations with Hudson, least of all ones involving the two of them.

'I'm heading overseas to work,' she said, enunciating each word with precision. 'And unlike what you implied, I won't be lying on my back with my legs spread to do it.'

'Don't be crass.'

'You're the one who seems to think I'm capable of it.'

To her horror, all the emotion she'd managed to subdue in front of him for the last few days bubbled up and lodged in her throat, making her nauseous.

'I have to go.' She slipped into her car and tried to slam the door shut.

He wouldn't budge. 'Hudson, I mean it—'

'I'm not letting you go,' he ground out. 'I've made that mistake several times now but never again.'

She gaped at him, letting the implications of his words sink in, totally missing her chance to shut the door and drive away when he moved around to the passenger side and slid into the seat next to her.

'Do you want to have this conversation here or somewhere more comfortable?'

Makayla didn't reply. For the simple reason she didn't know what to say. But whatever he had to say, she didn't want to be twisted like a pretzel in her tiny car, eyeing him while he divulged whatever declaration he had to make.

Her heart thudded out of control as she managed to start the engine and steer the car out onto the road.

'Where are we going?'

She shot him a sideways glance. 'You'll find out.'

Thankfully, he didn't say anything, content to let her drive. Then again, he'd said enough.

'I'm not letting you go...never again.'

What the hell did he mean by that?

She couldn't take him to her place, in case Charlotte was home. And she felt foolish driving to his apartment after the way things had ended between them. So she settled for her favourite spot when she wanted to get away from life.

Fifteen minutes later, she'd parked in secluded bushland on top of a cliff, with magnificent views of the harbour.

'This is my favourite go-to place and if you tell anyone it's here I'll have to kill you,' she said, finally breaking the silence.

'It's beautiful.' He swivelled his body to face her, moonlight illuminating the chiselled planes of his cheeks, his jaw. 'It's perfect.'

'For what?'

'Starting the rest of our lives.'

He pronounced it like a *fait accompli* as once again she struggled to gain control of her galloping heart.

'I think I've missed something,' she said, her voice sounding way too quivery. 'We're over and I'm heading to New York. What part of that screams a long-lasting relationship to you?'

'The part where I love you and have been too proud or too stupid to tell you.' He clasped her hand where it rested on her gearshift. 'The part where I tell you why I freak out every time I think of you trying to make it on your own.' He lifted her hand to his lips and brushed a feather-light kiss across the back of it. 'The part where I tell you I'll do whatever it takes to be with you. Quit my job. Follow you to New York. To the ends of the bloody earth if needs be, to ensure we're together.'

The blood drained from Makayla's head, making her woozy. Nothing about this evening made sense, starting with her crappy performance and culminating in this surreal moment, where the guy she'd fallen for was vowing to follow her to maintain their relationship.

'I'm having a hard time computing this,' she admitted, confusion making her brain hurt. 'I just don't get it.'

'I visited my father yesterday. Learned a few things that helped me put things in perspective.' He threaded his fingers through hers and held on tight, as if he'd never let go. 'I don't want any secrets between us. You need to know everything before we go any further.'

'Okay,' she said, the gravity in his tone making her wonder what deep, dark secret he had to reveal and how it would impact them.

'That night I saw you strip and I freaked out? It wasn't only because I'd worked around Kings Cross and seen women on a slippery slope.' He half turned and stared out of the window. 'It's because it happened to my mum. We had no money, stripping paid well, so she ended up in that profession. I learned yesterday my dad virtually pushed her into it then despised her for it, making it untenable for her to stay around so she left. I was six at the time. I lost my mum and it devastated me. When I saw you stripping, I didn't want to lose you too.'

Shocked, she sucked in a breath. Poor Hudson. No wonder he'd had a coronary when he'd seen her that night.

'When I was sixteen, I wanted to find Mum and I traced her to Melbourne. Took the train down there. Followed a bunch of leads and finally found her.' He swallowed and locked gazes with her, the agony in his eyes making her chest ache. 'Dead. In a bedsit, from a drug overdose. She'd been prostituting to support her habit—'

His voice broke, and she leaned across the console to wrap her arms around him. How had they been best friends and she'd known nothing of this? Of the kind of heartache that shaped a young man and made him fear anything remotely resembling an emotional commitment?

'I never told anyone,' he murmured, clinging to her, before gently easing back. 'But I'm sorry I let all that affect our friendship back then and how I treated you when I heard you were heading to New York.'

'It's okay, I get it now.'

And she did. Hudson wasn't the narrow-minded, overbearing, possessive prick she'd assumed. He was a guy scarred by his past and concerned for her welfare because of it.

'But I'm not going to earn money that way ever again. It's a promise I made to myself after that one night.' Her nose crinkled like she'd smelled something bad. 'I couldn't handle it and I wouldn't do it for anyone else but Mum. So you can rest assured I won't fall into disrepute in New York so you don't have to follow me there—'

'I do.' He reached for both her hands and held them. 'I love you. I want to be with you. And I've wasted enough years we could've been together by my own misconceptions.'

The heaviness that had weighed her down during her performance tonight lifted. 'That's twice you've said you love me. Must be real.'

'And you haven't said it once.' A glimmer of a smile played about his mouth. 'Does that mean you don't feel the same way?'

'Don't be an idiot, of course I love you.' She slipped a hand from his to thump him on the chest. 'I love you so much. There's a difference between not giving up my independence and dreams for any man, and giving up the man of my dreams.'

'Poetic,' he said, a moment before he claimed her mouth in a sizzling kiss that branded her as his. Or maybe it was the other way around.

Their tongues tangled, sinuous and hot, as he moved his lips over hers in that commanding way she loved.

He groaned into her mouth, his hands finding her breasts. She arched into him. Wanting him to touch her everywhere. She'd missed him, missed this. This way of making her feel like she was the only woman in the world for him. After his honest declaration, maybe she was.

He tried to get closer to her and thunked his head

on the car roof. 'Damn, not enough room,' he said with a rueful grin.

Her body throbbed with wanting him and her panties were soaked. No way were they leaving here without getting the happy ending they both wanted.

'There's always the back seat?' She quirked an eyebrow in a saucy invitation, and he laughed.

'You're serious?'

'Unless you want to wait 'til we get back to your place—'

'Back seat it is,' he said, already clambering over the console with a few bumps, curses and grunts.

She all but tumbled into his lap in her haste to follow, and they laughed in a tangle of limbs.

'How many times have you brought a boy up here to make out in the back seat?'

'As of now, only one.' She settled herself on his lap, anticipation making her crazy for him.

'So I'm your one and only? I like the sound of that.'

He flicked his thumbs across her nipples, rigid beneath the leotard she hadn't changed out of in her haste to escape the club.

She moaned, and he fastened his mouth where his thumb had been a moment ago, giving a sharp nip that made her grab his head and hold on.

As his teeth continued to torture her nipples to the point of exquisite pleasure, she heard him unzip. Heard the rip of foil. Felt his fingers pull aside her panties.

Then finally, finally, he was inside her. Hard and thick and perfect.

His mouth released her nipple, only to claim her lips

again, his tongue mimicking the demanding thrusts of his cock below.

Bracing her arms against the back seat, she rode him with abandon. Pumping up and down as if she'd never get enough. Every slide making her muscles tense. Every thrust bringing release closer.

The car filled with murmured pleas for satisfaction. Naughty demands. Each and every word bringing her closer to tumbling into the dazzling abyss she craved with his every touch.

Soon their frantic panting was the only sound in the car, the fogged windows enclosing them in their own private pleasure cave. Then he touched her clit, circling it, and she couldn't hold back any longer. Her orgasm crashed over her in a cataclysmic wave, making her see stars in the darkness.

Hudson grabbed her waist, anchoring her in a world where she floated; weightless, boneless, mindless with pleasure.

He thrust upward one last time before groaning her name, so raw, so guttural; she'd never heard anything so beautiful.

Crushing her to him, he didn't move, didn't speak.

No words were necessary.

They'd said all that needed to be said.

Hudson loved her. She loved him.

He wanted to foster her dream, not tear it down.

And they'd just sealed their love in the best way possible.

How the hell did she get so lucky?

EPILOGUE

AFTER THE ROUSING send-off Tanner had hosted for them at Embue last night, Hudson hadn't expected the gang to turn up at the airport to farewell them.

But Tanner, Abby and Charlotte had fronted up twenty-four hours later, in the wee small hours, to share a final drink.

'Here's to Mak taking Broadway by storm.' Tanner raised a beer. 'And to my putz of a friend not hanging on to her coat-tails like some dweeb.'

'I'll drink to that.' Mak clinked her champagne flute against Tanner's beer and winked at Hudson. 'Don't worry, darling, I'm fine with you tagging along for the ride.'

Hudson shot Abby a sympathetic look. 'I have no idea how you put up with this idiot.'

'It's a tough job, but somebody's got to do it.' Abby leaned her head against Tanner's shoulder, totally smitten, batting her eyelashes at Hudson's friend who dropped a kiss on the tip of her nose.

'Sickening,' Hudson muttered, unable to hide a goofy grin as he locked gazes with Tanner and he saw the same starstruck gleam reflected in his.

They'd been through so much growing up in Kings Cross. Had survived the tough streets and tougher fathers. Now look how far they'd come. Abby and Mak were beautiful, intelligent and talented in their respective fields, and they adored them.

'How did schmucks like us get so lucky?' Tanner asked, reading his mind.

'No idea, but I'm eternally frigging grateful.' Hudson clinked his beer against Tanner's, counting his blessings daily that he had a woman like Mak in his life.

'If I'd known this would be one giant love-fest, I never would've tagged along,' Charlotte said, poking her tongue out. 'I'm happy for you guys, but you make me sick.'

'Aww, honey.' Mak slipped an arm around her friend's waist. 'You'll meet someone soon.'

'Yeah, and I'll be sitting alongside the pilot flying your plane too.' Charlotte rolled her eyes. 'No offence, Hudson and Tanner, but men are the pits.'

Hating Charlotte's morose expression, Hudson proposed a toast. 'To Charlotte. A wonderful woman who needs to find some bozo like us to rip the blinkers from his eyes.'

'To Charlotte.' They chorused in unison, and Hudson was relieved when she mouthed 'thank you' at him.

Mak tapped her bottom lip, making Hudson hard in an instant. With a little luck and a lot of manoeuvring in a tight space, he might get to join the mile-high club shortly.

'You know, Char, I predict you'll have some hottie wrapped around your finger by the time we come back for a visit in six months.' Mak nudged Abby. 'I'm counting on you to help her find said hottie, okay?'

'Poor you,' Charlotte said to Abby. 'Hasn't happened in twenty-six years, can't see it happening in six months.'

Abby glared at Mak. 'Don't put that kind of pressure on her.'

Hudson bit back a laugh. What Abby really meant was, 'Don't put that kind of pressure on me.'

Mak grinned and blew Abby a kiss. 'I'm going to miss you.'

'You're going to miss my pastries, more like it.' Abby sounded curt, but Hudson saw the glint of tears in her eyes.

Great. Just what he needed when he wanted to whisk his girlfriend away: three blubbering women.

Intent on circumventing any potential waterworks, he raised his beer again. 'To us. Following dreams and following our hearts.'

They echoed his toast, and as Abby, Tanner and Charlotte engaged in a heated debate about online dating sites and their validity for finding long-lasting happiness, Hudson leaned into Mak.

'Ready to embrace your future?'

'With you, always.' She snuggled into his side, warm and loving, where she belonged.

This amazing woman wasn't the only one ready to embrace the future. He had no idea what it might bring but as long as he had Mak, he was ready to face it, head-on.

* * * * *

COMING SOON!

We really hope you enjoyed reading this book. If you're looking for more romance, be sure to head to the shops when new books are available on

Thursday 26th July

To see which titles are coming soon, please visit **millsandboon.co.uk**

LET'S TALK *Romance*

For exclusive extracts, competitions and special offers, find us online:

- facebook.com/millsandboon
- @millsandboonuk
- @millsandboon

Or get in touch on 0844 844 1351*

For all the latest titles coming soon, visit millsandboon.co.uk/nextmonth

*Calls cost 7p per minute plus your phone company's price per minute access charge